I0789027

# TRAFALGAR & BOONE AT MAGIC'S END

### Book Six of Trafalgar and Boone

Geonn Cannon

Supposed Crimes LLC • Matthews, North Carolina

Published in the United States.

ISBN: 978-1-952150-08-1

www.supposedcrimes.com

This book is typeset in Goudy Old Style.

When we last visited our intrepid heroes...

DOROTHY BOONE and MISS TRAFALGAR defeated the revived Forty Elephants gang, but at a tremendous cost.

ABRAHAM STRODE, a founding member of the MNEMOSYNE SOCIETY, is dead. IVY SEVER seems to have fled London entirely. But the most crushing loss is that of BEATRICE SEK, whose overuse of magic has left her lying comatose in the master bedroom of Dorothy's Threadneedle Street townhouse with no guarantee that she will ever recover. The remaining Elephants have joined the Mnemosyne Society as apprentices, to be mentored by existing members to learn how to control and take full advantage of their uncanny abilities.

The events have left Dorothy and Trafalgar shaken. Having seen what a loss of magic has done to their beloved Beatrice, they have decided to heed the warning of RIYA LENNOX and do everything in their power to help curb the widespread use of magic.

But in a world of ever-increasing danger, can they truly turn their back on such a valuable resource? And will they agree on exactly how far is too far?

## PROLOGUE

AT SOME point, Beatrice Sek discovered she could rise from her bed. So when the boredom of her condition came over her, she went for a wander around the house.

She wasn't sleeping, so she couldn't say she awoke. Those in the house couldn't see her but they occasionally seemed aware of her passage. Time didn't matter in the place in which she'd found herself. The light coming in through the windows was a murky blend of dawn and dusk, a pale glow just barely bright enough to see by. The halls and stairwells were full of blurs that she quickly realized were Dorothy Boone and Trafalgar moving over the course of several years. She could see a clear path where Dorothy moved from bed to the washroom to the library, down to the parlor, into the kitchen, out the door, a journey taken many times with little variation. Trafalgar was a solid presence in her reading chair due to how many hours were spent there, and moving slowly along the shelves as she searched the spines of books, and she was a twitching body with blurred arms and legs in the study where she trained in various fighting styles.

Beatrice saw herself as well. Cleaning, cooking, patrolling. She saw herself frozen in the vault, a thief trapped in stone waiting for Dorothy to come rescue her. Guests weren't as dominant, mere wisps among the kaleidoscope of the house's three occupants living their lives. She saw Desmond Tindall, though his paths were becoming depressingly faint.

She could only make out the finer details of her friends and lovers in the places they spent the most time. Dorothy at her desk, though her face and fingers were a blur. Trafalgar in bed, sleeping in a handful of repeated and predictable positions. Conversations were a low buzz, every word ever spoken in the house echoing like the roar of an ocean.

And then she saw Dorothy, sat beside the bed where Beatrice's body lay, so still and defined that it was almost as if she was a statue. She must have spent hours in that chair barely moving. Keeping watch. Sometimes carrying on a one-sided conversation, if the blur around her mouth was any indication. Beatrice tried touching Dorothy's hand, her face, her hair, but Dorothy never seemed to notice. Trafalgar sat with her as well, but nowhere nearly as often. That was fine. Beatrice didn't want them to put their lives on hold for her. It was bad enough one of them was wasting so many hours in this room.

So Beatrice watched the specter of Dorothy, the remnant of visiting the same spot day upon day and not moving until exhaustion or hunger forced her to her feet.

Dorothy watched the body in the bed, while its spirit sat on the other side of the mattress to watch over her. Beatrice didn't mind.

Time didn't mean the same thing here, and there was nothing in the world she would rather be doing.

Sometimes she could hear their voices. There was a day, one day, when the downstairs parlor was full of people who rarely spent time in the house, so their footprint was much easier to pin down. She saw them in a single outfit, staying in one space, with blurred movements to indicate hand gestures or sipping from a tea cup. Beatrice haunted this room until she determined the low buzzing noise was conversation. She recognized the voices and spent time isolating them. She had no idea how long she spent doing this, because technically she spent no time at all. She remained in the seconds of a single afternoon, living them repeatedly until they solidified like gelatin. It was still a bit wobbly, but it had substance. She could line up the words until they were spoken in the correct order.

Agnes and Leonard Keeping, the eldest members of the Society but still dangerously dapper, were posted by the fireplace. Leonard wore a waistcoat with no jacket. His wife wore a striped blouse with a high collar, her wild curls pinned up in a complicated do.

"Is this really the best way to go about this?" Agnes asked. "We're dividing these poor women up like chattel. They're human beings. They should have a right to say where they end up."

Trafalgar, who seemed to be in charge of the meeting, was in Dorothy's wingback chair. Beatrice knew they were discussing the remaining members of the Forty Elephants gang of thieves.

"The sad truth is, their only other option is prison. They actively participated in an untold number of crimes, up to and including murder. Their saving grace is that, for the most part, they're showing remorse for their actions. They want to make amends. Scotland Yard agrees with me that apprenticing with the Mnemosyne Society is the best chance at rehabilitating them."

Cecil Dubourne, standing at the window with a shoulder against the wall, scoffed. He wore a rumpled shirt untucked over tartan pants, and his hair was too shaggy to be fashionable. "Scotland Yard knows there ain't no way to hold onto these lasses even if they wanted to. There's one of 'em who can make herself look like any of the guards. And at least one can just punch down a brick wall. The police aren't doing anyone a kindness. They're letting us take away their headache."

"Whatever their motives," Trafalgar said, "we owe it to these women to help them however we can."

Cecil raised a finger. "Point of order, most of *them* tried to kill at least some of *us*."

"That will be taken into account," Trafalgar said.

Cora was in the center of the divan, back straight and hands folded in her lap. "What exactly are you proposing, Trafalgar?"

Trafalgar said, "Apprenticing. We will make them honorary members of the Society. We'll each be responsible for a certain number of the women. They'll assist us on missions and in return, we'll educate them about using their abilities responsibly."

"All of us...?" Cora glanced at Cecil.

Cecil made a rude gesture in response.

Trafalgar said, "Mr. Dubourne is actually an important component. I said that *most* of them are remorseful about what they did in the employ of Maud Keaton. Others are more reluctant to give up the life of crime. Those are the women who will be entrusted to his care."

Leonard made a noise of disbelief. "A bit like locking the fox in the henhouse, don't you think?"

"For all of his faults, Mr. Dubourne is a decent man. He does good, in his own way. Dorothy has watched him carefully over the years, and she knows his expeditions are respectful of the dead and their cultures. I believe the women will respond positively to his, shall we say, lenient approach to rules and propriety. He will be an example that being good doesn't necessarily mean being boring."

Cecil squared his shoulders. "I hope someone wrote that down. I want that exact same thing said at my funeral."

Trafalgar ignored him. She pulled out a notebook and placed it on the table. "I've taken the liberty of drawing up a list. Three groups, ten each. Except for you, Cora, who will have eleven. I apologize, but there were twins..."

"Perfectly fine," Cora said.

Cecil said, "Three groups? Me, the geezers, and Missus Hyde? You and Boone ain't takin' none of 'em, when this was your bloody idea?"

Cora said, "Dorothy and Trafalgar are already dealing with their own crisis. They can't be expected to also accept responsibility for a whole gaggle of young women who need guidance."

Trafalgar nodded. "We'll also serve as a backup option. There are a lot of big personalities in this group." She tapped the paper, then gestured around the room. "And in this group. I have to anticipate there will be disagreements and scuffles. If anyone can't make it work with their mentor, they will come to me and Dorothy so as not to add an extra burden on one of the other groups."

Cecil grunted and let the argument drop.

"Where will these women be staying?" Cora asked. "I don't think any of us have the necessary room to accommodate ten new boarders."

Agnes answered before Trafalgar could speak. "There's a boardinghouse near our place. It would need a lot of work, but maybe the girls could make that part of their rehabilitation. Earn their keep by sprucing up the place."

"Makes sense to me," Cora said.

"Splendid." Trafalgar had made copies of the list and handed them out to everyone. "The women will be waiting for us at the Inkwell in an hour. I've given them copies of this list as well, and none of them objected to their placement. If anyone here has objections, I'd be happy to hear them out." She looked around, but no one spoke up. Trafalgar nodded and pushed herself up out of the chair. "Then let's go meet our new apprentices, hm?"

The Society members slowly drifted out of the room. To Beatrice, it was like they simply faded out of existence. Only Trafalgar remained solid, an anchor in time, her face lit by sun coming in from the window. Beatrice touched her cheek. Trafalgar smiled, closed her eyes as if trying to identify the source of a half-heard song, and then shook off the strange feeling.

"I'll check on you soon, Trix. I promise."

She passed through Beatrice's spirit on the way out of the room but Beatrice was the one who shivered.

There were other days she could visit, moments of calm and quiet where she could pretend everything was normal. Mostly she waited, wandered, listened, remembered.

Something would happen. A change was coming, and it would be here soon. She could feel it like fog rolling in from offshore, creating sudden darkness of a summer afternoon. She only hoped she was able to help when it finally arrived.

## CHAPTER ONE

**1923**

DOROTHY DOZED off sometime around four in the morning and woke only when she heard Trafalgar's soft footsteps in the hall. She sat up and straightened her clothes, twisted to see the clock so she'd know what time it was, and looked at the bed to see if there was any change in Beatrice's condition. It was hardly the first time she'd fallen asleep here in the past few months, and it didn't matter how long she slept. This vigil was her priority; nothing else mattered.

The door opened enough for Trafalgar to peek in before she entered. She was dressed in a button-down shirt, brown pants, suspenders, and boots. She carried a teacup in one hand, a plate of sausage, eggs, toast, and jam in the other.

"You're awake," she said.

Dorothy squared her shoulders. "I've been awake all night."

"Then I'm very annoyed with you for ignoring me when I came in to wish you a good morning."

Dorothy twisted her lips. "I was awake. I... had nothing to say."

Trafalgar said, "Then you were dreaming, because this is the first time I've been in here since yesterday."

Dorothy was uncertain which was the lie, and grunted at being found out. She angrily tugged at the cuffs of her blouse. "I don't appreciate being tricked."

Trafalgar held out the breakfast. "You're only cross because you haven't eaten anything since tea time yesterday."

Dorothy considered ignoring it, but the food smelled divine and she really was starved. She took the plate with a muttered thank-you, placing the tea on the bedside table.

Trafalgar sat on the edge of the bed and slipped her hand into Beatrice's. They had long ago stopped asking each other for updates on her condition. No change, for better or worse. It had been over eight months since the assault on the Elephants' stronghold. Everyone else's wounds had long healed, but Beatrice remained the same as when she was pulled out of the Compter Comfort House where Maud Keaton had made her headquarters.

Whatever blow felled her, it hadn't been physical. The doctors Dorothy brought in all agreed Beatrice was healthy. No trauma, bleeding on the brain, or anything else that might account for her condition. There was no doubt that she was suffering from overexertion of her magical abilities. Apparently there was only so much energy she could draw before the tank ran dry, and she'd hit that bottom and tried to keep going. She had been using her powers not only for the assault, but to protect the townhouse... both things Dorothy had asked her to do.

This was her fault. If Beatrice died because of her...

She silenced that train of thought before it could go any further. Since then, Beatrice had remained here in the master bedroom of the townhouse. Dorothy slept in Beatrice's room on the rare nights she was convinced to lie down for a few hours. She had lost weight and was beginning to look a bit haggard even by her own assessment. She knew she needed to take better care of herself, but every moment she spent away from Beatrice felt like a betrayal.

As a compromise, she picked up one of the sausages Trafalgar had brought her. It only took a few bites to realize how hungry she was. She ate everything too quickly to pretend she wasn't grateful, and she nodded her thanks. Trafalgar had the good grace to not gloat, and simply stroked the back of Beatrice's hand until Dorothy was finished with her meal.

She put the empty plate aside, sipped her tea, and blotted her lips with a napkin. "Thank you."

"You're welcome. There's more downstairs, if you wish. But you have to go get it yourself."

Dorothy looked at Beatrice's deceptively peaceful face. "I can't."

Trafalgar sighed and nodded, an acknowledgement if not acceptance. "Very well. I didn't come up here just to bring you breakfast. Leonard and Agnes Keeping have asked me to come by for a visit. I believe they wish to invite me on an expedition with them."

Dorothy was startled. "Do you intend to accept?"

Trafalgar sighed. "It has been months since we've done anything of substance. We study, we spar, we wander these halls, waiting for something to happen with our dear Trix. At some point, life must go on. I believe

Beatrice would agree with me on that."

Dorothy clenched her teeth, her jaw working as she stared down at the teacup in her hands. "I can't go with you. I won't."

"I understand."

"The day I met her," Dorothy said, "she had been imprisoned in stone for weeks. Conscious, aware, and alone. I can't imagine what that might have done to her. I would have been driven mad. I don't know if she's aware of what's happening to her now, but when she wakes, I want to be here. I need to tell her I was by her side as much as possible."

Trafalgar said, "At some point you will have to—"

"At some point, yes!" Dorothy snapped, harsher than she intended, and she sagged when she saw the surprised lift of Trafalgar's eyebrows. "Not now," Dorothy said quietly. "Not yet."

"All right." Trafalgar stood and bent down to kiss Dorothy's cheek. "I miss you."

"I miss you as well," Dorothy said. "But it's supposed to be the three of us. It doesn't..."

"I know. I agree. But I wanted to have it said." She stroked Dorothy's hair. "I am going to see the Keepings, and then I will come back to sit with her so you can get some rest. Don't bother arguing with me. It's a battle you'll lose. It should only take an hour or so."

Dorothy twisted her lips, looking to one side so she wouldn't have to meet Trafalgar's gaze. "As you wish."

Trafalgar straightened and looked at the bed. "I'll see you soon, Beatrice."

She left the room, and Dorothy waited until she heard the downstairs door close before she rose from the chair. She put the empty cup on the saucer, then pulled back the blankets to join Beatrice in bed. If she was going to be forced to sleep, this might be a compromise she could live with. She put her head on Beatrice's shoulder and closed her eyes, knowing she would wake if the other woman stirred even a little.

Trafalgar donned a bowler hat before she left the house. She found cloche hats very attractive, but the low brim limited her visibility to an unacceptable level. Unfortunately going without a hat was not an option. The citizens of London had been slow to accept an African woman of her height wearing fine clothing and casually strolling along Threadneedle Street, and shaving her head only made her more of a peculiarity. People still gawped at her when she passed, but it was impossible to tell if their shock was for her height, race, gender, or wardrobe. She could live with the uncertainty.

The day was nice enough that she opted to walk to the Keepings' house. It was a little over four miles, but the meeting wasn't until noon, and she wanted to give Dorothy a little extra time before rushing her off to bed. The honest truth was that she desperately wanted to be doing exactly as Dorothy was doing. Her mind was never far from the room that had become a shrine to their fallen friend. She thought of Adeline's tragic end. In a way it had been a blessing. Quick, brutal, final. Trafalgar felt in her heart that Beatrice was equally lost to them, but she still had a heartbeat. The doctors who tended to her insisted she was alive, merely in a deep comatose state.

Trafalgar feared the day would come soon when that changed. But until then, letting Dorothy spend every waking hour at her side couldn't do much harm. At least she prayed it couldn't.

The Keepings lived in a lovely terraced home just south of Hyde Park. She barely had time to lower her fist from knocking before the red door swung open to reveal the disheveled countenance of Leonard Keeping. His version of scruffiness, of course, would seem tidy on a lesser man. It was only because she knew him so well that she took note of his rumpled collar, the hint of pale white whiskers on his jawline, and the bags beneath his eyes.

Despite this, his smile was warm and welcoming. "Miss Trafalgar!" He glanced at the street. "Lady Boone didn't accompany you?"

"She was indisposed. We could reschedule, if..."

"No, of course not. You can relay any information she may need." He stepped aside. "Please, please, come in."

Trafalgar removed her hat as she entered the home. He took it from her and placed it on the rack at the foot of the stairs. Music drifted from the library at the far end of the hall, and seemed to carry with it an unusual fragrance. Leonard rested his hand briefly on her arm as he passed her; she took it as a hint that she was supposed to follow him.

"Agnes is in the library. We're having a very exciting weekend."

"I believe you'll find it's Tuesday, Mr. Keeping."

He slowed and considered that, then nodded once. "I suppose it is! Interesting." He laughed and raised his eyebrows at her. "Quite a weekend indeed, you can see."

Trafalgar couldn't resist smiling at his excitement. She had always enjoyed the Keepings. He was stodgy, absent-minded, and infinitely curious in both senses of the word. He seemed most at home in a library but was imminently capable of wielding a broadsword or flintlock pistol if the need arose. His other half, Agnes, gave the appearance of a scholarly professor, the type who blended into the shelving of a college library, constantly shrouded in tweed and the dust of some ancient manuscript. While this was partially accurate, Agnes was her husband's equal in every way, and Trafalgar would be reluctant to place money on either of them in a fair fight. Barehanded or with weapons, both of the Keepings could do considerable damage before the final bell rang.

Simply put, Leonard and Agnes displayed brains and brawn in

measures that made them champions of both, and both strengths were put to shame by their kindness.

Agnes looked up when Trafalgar entered and half-smiled, nodded her head, and put down the book she was referencing. She took off her reading glasses, tucked her silver hair behind her ears, and came around the table to greet their guest properly. She put a hand on Trafalgar's shoulder and leaned in to lightly kiss both of her cheeks.

"Hello, Miss Trafalgar. Thank you for coming at such an inconvenient time."

Trafalgar squeezed Agnes' arm. "I'm always available for another founding member of the Mnemosyne Society. But that is especially true for you and Leonard." She looked at the vast array of reference books and maps spread across the table. "Whatever you have brewing is bound to be worth the trip."

"Brewing," Leonard said, eyes wide as he realized his gaffe. "Goodness. We didn't offer you tea or... have you eaten? I don't even know if we have... We can get~"

"I'm not hungry. Although if you would happen to have a glass of water..." He hurried off to get it, gone before she could offer her thanks.

Agnes chuckled. "Excuse him. We're both a bit giddy from long nights."

"He didn't seem to know it was Tuesday."

"Is it!" Agnes said. "I would have sworn Monday, but... no, that makes sense." She reached up to touch her missing glasses, covered the move by patting her hair. "Ah. We may need a moment to, ahem, to gather our thoughts so we can properly tell you why you've been summoned. Lady Boone? Is she on her way, or...?"

"No, she won't be able to make it."

"Ah, short notice. No matter." She hurried back to the table. "I was hoping to thank her - and you as well! - for introducing us to those lovely young women. The newest members of the Society."

Trafalgar smiled. "So the former Elephants have proven helpful to you?"

Agnes wrinkled her nose. "I don't care for that moniker. Although it is how I've heard them refer to each other, so I suppose..." She waved off that topic. "The fact of the matter is that Dorothy was absolutely correct. Once the girls were given a bit of guidance, all they truly wanted was a place to fit in. They're not averse to hard work, as Leonard and I have put to the test. They exceed our expectations at every turn."

"Where are they now?"

"Where are who?" Leonard returned at that moment with a glass of water and a biscuit wrapped in a napkin. Trafalgar smiled and nodded to him, winking in thanks as she slipped the snack into her pocket.

"The girls. That's part of what we wish to discuss with you." She seemed almost giddy with excitement and looked at her husband. "Would you like to tell her?"

Leonard gestured for her to go on. "You've brought us this far, my dear."

Agnes' eyes sparkled and she patted her hand on the table. "This, my dear Trafalgar, is our white whale. It's what Leonard and I have been seeking since we first got into this profession. Earlier, even!"

"It was the quest that brought us together," Leonard said.

"And by that measure, it has already proven to be invaluable," Agnes said with a smile. "But the value to the world at large is likely to be immeasurable. What do you know of Seaxburh, the Queen consort of Wessex?"

Trafalgar said, "Precisely everything you've just told me about her. Beyond that..."

Leonard laughed. "You can be forgiven. She was married to the Anglo-Saxon King Cenwalh until his death in 672, at which point she became his successor."

"An Anglo-Saxon Queen?" Trafalgar said. "I've never heard of such a thing."

"They were exceedingly rare, and some deny their existence at all," Agnes said. "I've always believed she truly existed. She only reigned for a year, perhaps two, but she's largely ignored by Bede because he was a misogynistic Mrs. Grundy who probably couldn't bear to list a woman as a leader."

"Dear..." Leonard chided. "Bede wrote very little about Wessex in general, or Mercia..."

"Yes, yes, I'm sure he just forgot to include the first female ruler. It slipped his mind. Regardless of why she was either ignored or erased from the public record, the fact remains that she existed. I first heard about her when I was at university and I made it my quest to discover her final resting place. You can imagine there's not much in the way of information about her, so when I discovered an ancient log of Wessex rulers was going up for auction, I gathered all my savings to get my hands on it. Unfortunately, some blowhard from Oxford had similar ideas."

Leonard smiled. "I wasn't looking for information on Seaxburh, of course. I had other interests for which the log would be extremely useful. I made the journey expecting to get it for cheap. I couldn't imagine anyone else being interested in it."

Agnes said, "Not the first time you've underestimated me."

"And we're still years away from the last, I'm certain."

"Well, who won?"

Leonard rolled his eyes. "Need you ask?"

"He caught up with me outside the auction house and offered the full amount of his final bid in exchange for one afternoon with the book. I insisted the visit be supervised, and I watched as he furiously copied what he needed. I believe I may have distracted him with conversation so I offered to come back the following day at no extra charge."

"With ulterior motives, I'm certain," Trafalgar said coyly.

"My intentions were pure."

"You forgot to bring the book the second time!" Leonard said. "She seduced me as a distraction, so I would lose interest in trying to steal away her prize."

Agnes waved away his protest. "We're getting off topic. The point is this: the log started me on the path to locating Seaxburh of Wessex's final resting place. And now, after all these years of searching..." She beamed, looking as young as she must have been on the day she first heard the story. "We've found her, Trafalgar."

## CHAPTER TWO

"THE GIRLS have been a godsend," Agnes said as she spread a map across the table. "We chose a small group to be our vanguard at the site, and they've performed leaps and bounds above our expectations. The amount of work they're able to do is nothing short of astonishing. Sadie Halladay is a sprite. She can run the length of the Thames in two minutes, but I was positive she wouldn't be able to retain anything she tried to read at that pace. She proved me woefully wrong."

"Violet Rhys also proved crucial to the goal," Leonard said. "She calls her ability 'faraway eyes.' Show her a place on the map and she can see it in her mind in its current state. Saves us a fair bit of travel expenses, you can imagine. We were able to track down resources, follow leads, and eliminate dead ends without ever leaving the house."

Agnes jabbed her finger at the map. "All this time and she was just over a hundred miles away from us in Suffolk. Violet saw her buried in a ship beneath a hill. A ship-burial would make sense for someone of her stature."

"Or," Leonard said, "someone who believed herself worthy of such an honor."

"She was a queen," Trafalgar said. "Surely she deserved a ruler's burial."

Agnes said, "There's some debate on that matter, whether she was a powerful ruler or despised by her people. Some say she was a beloved queen. Others say she was a madwoman with delusions of grandeur who usurped the throne. It truly depends on which source you choose to believe. While we have no evidence she was a poor leader~"

"Other than the fact she held the throne for less than two years," Leonard interjected.

"We know she was capable of securing the throne for herself when her husband had a brother who could have taken over instead. Anyone capable of taking a crown under such circumstances and holding it, even for a short time, would have to be a cunning thinker."

Leonard said, "Or a dictator, a despot, a–"

"How *dare*...!"

Trafalgar cleared her throat. "I assume none of this is pertinent to the burial site."

"Yes, my apologies." Agnes touched her hair as if her anger had caused it to burst free from its binding. "As you can probably tell, we've been going back and forth on this for quite some time. We now believe beyond a shadow of a doubt that Seaxburh was laid to rest in a ship, and the location is in Suffolk. If we can find it and see what she was buried with, we will have more evidence as to how she was regarded by contemporaries, rather than relying on the accounts of men who lived six hundred years after her."

"Beyond that," Leonard said, "if the artifacts are well-preserved, they'll be an unprecedented glimpse into a long-ago past."

Trafalgar said, "Well, you've certainly piqued my interest. What do you require from us?"

"The girls, the Elephants, are in Suffolk as we speak trying to secure the land for our excavation. Once we've been granted permission, we want you and Dorothy to be the first ones inside."

"I'm stunned," Trafalgar said. "After all this time, you would let someone else take the first step?"

Agnes said, "It's because of our history with the queen that we cannot be the ones who open the door. We may inadvertently damage something in our excitement. At the very least we can be certain to bring our personal biases to everything we see. If it's not actually the final resting place of Seaxburh, our brains may distort the facts to fit our beliefs. We trust you and Dorothy to be the ones who make this discovery."

"That's quite an honor." If Dorothy was unwilling to travel across town to take a lunch meeting, Trafalgar didn't expect a different answer for an overnight trip. "I must be honest, I don't know that Dorothy will be up to such an undertaking."

"Oh I see." Agnes furrowed her brow. "We asked for both of you because you seem joined at the hip. If only you are able to go, that would certainly more than enough. But now I'm a bit concerned. What ails the poor dear?"

Trafalgar was stunned. "Beatrice, of course."

Agnes blinked in surprise, then averted her eyes in shame. "Oh, goodness. Yes, of course. Of course. Oh. Forgive me."

Trafalgar pushed down her offense and irritation and nodded to accept the apology. "I'll discuss it with her. But if she refuses, I would be more than happy to go on my own. You've waited long enough for answers."

Agnes exhaled with sharp relief, nodding once. "Thank you."

"This conversation will be entirely academic if your girls aren't able to get permission to dig," Trafalgar said. "So I shall return home and talk this over with Dorothy, and you shall let me know if a trip is in order. I'll keep my schedule clear so we can begin immediately."

"You don't have to put your own work on hold for my mission," Agnes said.

Trafalgar shook her head. "On the contrary. I believe you've infected me with your zeal for the project."

Leonard smirked at his wife. "She has a way of doing that to people."

Beatrice opened her eyes. It took her a moment to realize the world was normal. Time passed in the traditional way, and the air wasn't full of past and future passage of other people. The house was quiet and the light was steady. Late morning or early afternoon. She blinked and sat up, aware of another body in the bed with her. She twisted and looked down to see...

Herself..

A dream. It had to be, it was the only explanation that made sense. After spending so long - weeks? Certainly not years... - in that strange Everytime place, this was just the next step. She lifted her hand to touch the cheek of the woman lying beside her to confirm it was real. She stopped before making contact, looked at the hand, realized it wasn't hers. The skin was the wrong color, for one. The phrase knowing something like the back of one's hand never rang so true. She also knew exactly who this hand belonged to.

"Crumbs."

She was wearing Dorothy's body. She looked down to confirm, then slipped out of bed and went to the mirror over the bureau. The face looking back at her was familiar, but the eyes were wrong. The lids drooped and her mouth was disturbingly slack. Beatrice touched her cheek, her bottom lip, and realized Dorothy's body was asleep.

"I'm sorry, Dorothy." The words came out in a slurred, sloppy grunt. Dorothy's voice sounded different in her head. "I would never do this to you on purpose. You've had enough people hijack your body to last a lifetime. I'll..."

She would what? Leave? But she felt conscious for the first time in... months, she was confident it had been months. Could she just step out and go back to the in-between state. But Dorothy didn't consent to this. The pharaoh taking over her body would have been traumatic even if that adventure hadn't ended in the death of Desmond Tindall. Beatrice refused to be an uninvited guest in the body of a woman she loved.

But perhaps she could communicate. Leave a note, or...

"Trafalgar!" She lurched toward the door, confused as to why Dorothy's body was so difficult to control. They weren't the same weight, though she imagined the difference had to be negligible. Dorothy was a bit taller, perhaps, and that might have been throwing her off. She was careful down the stairs, pausing at the landing to make sure Trafalgar wasn't in her room before moving down to the ground floor. The parlor was empty, as was the kitchen.

She was starting to get the hang of using Dorothy's legs to carry her around but she was still dragging her feet when the front door swung open.

Trafalgar entered, dapper in an overcoat and glaring hard from under the brim of her cap. She paused on the threshold, closed the door, and removed the cap before she started unbuttoning her jacket.

Dorothy startled awake at the sound of a door slamming directly in front of her. She groped blindly to one side, unsure of how she was standing up, and grabbed the banister before she tumbled to the ground. She looked around her in confusion as Trafalgar angrily shed her coat and hung it from a hook.

"I thought we agreed you would sleep."

"We... I-I was. I was sleeping." Dorothy touched her forehead to see if she was feverish. "I lay down next to Beatrice in the bed and fell asleep immediately. I dreamt... I had unusual dreams. And now I'm here." She looked at Trafalgar. "How long were you gone?"

Trafalgar seemed to believe her, as the anger had faded into concern. "Several hours." She put the back of her hand against Dorothy's cheek. "You don't feel feverish. Are you nauseated?"

"No. I don't think so. I'm unusually sore."

"Sleepwalking will do that to someone. Come with me into the parlor. You can sit and rest."

"I believe that would be wise."

Trafalgar put a hand across Dorothy's shoulders and guided her to the divan. They sat next to each other and Dorothy leaned against Trafalgar's side.

"I worry you're making yourself sick by pushing yourself this way," Trafalgar said softly. "It won't do Beatrice any good if you become bedridden. She wouldn't want that for you."

Dorothy nodded. "I know. But I can't... even a short trip out of the house is..." She closed her eyes and shook her head. "I'll try to sleep more regularly. And eat. But I cannot leave her. I won't abandon her."

"I suppose, if nothing else, that answers the question Leonard and Agnes wanted me to ask."

"The Keepings?"

"They hoped to enlist us for a mission."

She explained the story as best she knew how, and Dorothy listened carefully. Though she had apparently slept for hours, she still felt groggy. She managed to remain awake until Trafalgar finished speaking. When the story was done, Dorothy sat up straighter and nodded.

"It sounds like exactly the sort of adventure I need at the moment. But I can't. I won't."

Trafalgar squeezed Dorothy's arm. "How long do you expect to continue this way?"

"Until she wakes up."

"Dorothy..." Trafalgar looked down, then away. She'd practiced this conversation in her head dozens of times, but there was no way to approach it without risking Dorothy's ire. "Perhaps the time has come to consider getting her more professional care."

"We have physicians coming in every day," Dorothy said.

"You know what I'm saying."

Dorothy stood and started toward the stairs. "Yes, and I'm ignoring it for the sake of civility."

Trafalgar followed her. "She needs to be somewhere she can be properly cared for. If we don't make that decision soon, you will be sharing a room with her."

"How can you be so callous?" Dorothy growled, spinning to face her.

"I'm being practical," Trafalgar said softly, refusing to turn the conversation into a fight. "We must consider what's best for Beatrice. We're keeping her comfortable but if she was in a facility~"

"Poked, prodded, tested. We know what's wrong with her, and it's not something medicine can help her with. She needs magic."

Trafalgar bowed her head. "Please, Dorothy. Consider it."

Dorothy started to argue but then her shoulders slumped. "Fine. I will consider it, but only because we cannot continue having the same argument over and over again. We'll have an educated discussion about it at a later date when our heads are more settled." At this, she winced and touched her temple. Trafalgar stepped closer, but Dorothy waved her back. "No, no. It's nothing. Probably only requires some of that sleep you keep insisting I get. I'll go back upstairs and lie down."

"Would you like me to join you?"

"I think I would sleep better alone," Dorothy said with a smile. "But thank you for the offer."

"I hope you feel better soon."

Dorothy nodded her thanks and started upstairs. She turned on the third step. "You should accept the Keepings' invitation. You shouldn't miss such an extraordinary opportunity on my account."

Trafalgar smiled wryly. "Odd how you can say that with such sincerity, but can't imagine Beatrice saying the same thing to you."

"It is my lot in life to be contrary."

"Maddening," Trafalgar corrected.

"One woman's saint is another's sinner," Dorothy said.

Trafalgar said, "Pleasant dreams, Dorothy."

"Thank you, dear."

She went upstairs and closed the door of Beatrice's room behind her. She stretched out on top of the blankets, intending to lay there for an hour to appease Trafalgar's maternal clucking. It was lovely to have someone worried about her, even if it was a pain. The alternative was not having anyone to scold her for not taking care of herself, and who wanted that? It was hardly a life. So she would lie down, eyes closed, just to make Trafalgar happy. She knew she wouldn't be able to fall asleep even if she tried.

Beatrice looked down at Dorothy. She couldn't be sure if it was the Dorothy of the past or the one who lived now, the one she had just... what was the correct word? Possessed? Puppeteered? Time was unstuck again and in addition to the woman on the bed, she saw other Dorothys. Dressing, putting away laundry, reading in the armchair, and always the blurs of movement. She didn't know exactly how she had achieved the puppetry, but she was loathe to try it again. It had stolen valuable sleep time from Dorothy, as well as having a physical effect on her. Beatrice was certain the headache was her fault, and she whispered an apology just in case some version of Dorothy could hear it.

She swore to herself that she wouldn't try to take over anyone else's body, not unless it was an absolute emergency.

Or, she supposed, if she decided the time had come to finally say goodbye.

## CHAPTER THREE

SEVEN DAYS later, Trafalgar made the journey north to Suffolk. The Keeping girls had secured the land rights, and Agnes moved quickly to get everything in place to begin an immediate excavation. Trafalgar spent the train ride reading dossiers on the women she would be working with, handwritten biographies of each former Elephant provided by Leonard which included their abilities.

Trafalgar was overjoyed that their experiment had worked out so well. Even the members who had initially expressed hesitation to take on a group of former thieves and pickpockets had come to admit the Mnemosyne Society was much stronger with the new additions. Her main regret was that she and Dorothy hadn't taken in a group of their own, but Beatrice's condition had made that impossible. Trafalgar was eager to have a chance to see them in action for herself. It would be very gratifying to see how the reformed criminals had grown over the past few months.

When the train arrived, she gathered her things and waited on the platform for her ride. She had just checked her watch when she heard footsteps approaching from behind.

"I believe I'm your ride."

"Yes, so it would..."

The words died in Trafalgar's throat as she saw who it was. Thick curls of black hair framed her face underneath the brim of a straw boater. Her face was angular, full of sharp lines - cheeks, nose, jaw, smile - and dark eyes under thick eyebrows. She wore a black suit over a lightweight cotton shirt with a red bandana around her throat. The last time Trafalgar had seen this woman was during their assault of the Forty Elephants' stronghold.

"Zilla Beverly."

"You remember!" She pressed the fine-boned fingers of one hand to her chest. "I'm touched."

"I tend to remember people who promise I'll die at their hand."

Zilla raised an eyebrow. "Long list, izzit?"

"Longer than I'd like," Trafalgar said, "but full of people who failed and are unable to make a second attempt. Your name wasn't on the list I received from the Keepings."

"I asked Agnes not to tell you I was here. I wanted it to be a surprise." She stepped closer. "Are you surprised, Trafalgar?"

Trafalgar repositioned her left hand, bringing it closer to the knife on her hip. "I always relish the chance to tie up loose ends."

Zilla let the moment hang between them a moment longer before she relaxed the tension in her shoulders and held out an empty hand.

"I hold no grudge against you."

"You don't have a grudge against *me...?*" Trafalgar said.

Zilla curled her fingers but didn't withdraw her hand. "For invading our home and attacking my friends. Surely you understand how, from my perspective, you were the aggressor in that situation. I was merely protecting my sisters."

Trafalgar considered that version of events, then relaxed as well. There was no point in arguing her own point of view, and Maud Keaton had been their true adversary on that day. She took Zilla's hand, pumped it once, and let it go.

"Bygones. Anyone the Keepings trust as part of their team is worth a second chance in my book. So you actually *are* my ride?"

"I am." She bent to pick up Trafalgar's bag and led them back toward the lot. "I asked to be the one who came so we could have this little reunion privately. Just in case you were a bit irritated about working with someone you crossed fists with."

Trafalgar said, "If that was the case, I wouldn't be able to work with Lady Boone. People can change." She hesitated. "And just to put it on the record, you won our skirmish. I was unconscious and, had you so chosen, you could have ended my life. I would say that counts as a victory."

"Oh, I'm well aware." Zilla grinned, flashing a crooked tooth on the right side of her mouth. "But I wasn't going to rub your face in it on account of us bein' friends now." She loaded Trafalgar's bag into the cargo space of the car. "My abilities aren't particularly helpful in a research setting. No real need for someone who can produce paralyzing spikes from her skin when you're just reading books. But I can manage people real well. And I serve as security for the site. Feels real good being useful this way."

"I hope the other former Elephants feel the same way."

Zilla turned the ignition and pulled out onto the road. "Sadie,

Florence, and Violet definitely agree. They're the ones we'll be working with on the site. We've discussed it at length, and we all feel it's like getting an education without all the school. With Maud Keaton, we were just grabbing goodies. But with the Society, we're earning the things we have. And at the same time, we're making ourselves useful. Agnes thinks the world could be changed by what we find up here!"

Trafalgar smiled at the other woman's enthusiasm. "In a manner of speaking. Our *understanding* of the world will change, but to the general public, everything will continue unchanged."

"Well, even better. Now I feel like a member of the elite, knowing things only a select few get to know. That would make anyone feel proud."

"Indeed it should," Trafalgar said.

The drive took them out of the town and into a countryside of rolling hills, most spiked with trees while others were completely denuded and likely provided clear views for miles in every direction.

"I'm taking you straight to the site so we can introduce everyone to everyone," Zilla said, "and after that I'll take you to where we've been camping out. Let you get all settled in, nice and cozy."

"I appreciate it."

Zilla pulled onto a dirt road and parked next to a gap in a tumbling-down wooden fence. Two juniper trees stood on either side of the gate, which was standing open. They walked up the path together and Trafalgar could see the dig site long before they arrived at it. It was a perfectly nondescript, but absolutely idyllic, location. Stretches of pristine green hills rolled out in every direction as if created specifically for poets, painters, and picnickers.

The work was centered on one hill in particular. Trafalgar furrowed her brow when she saw nearly a dozen people milling around the site.

"I was told that only four of the Keepings' associates were working here, including yourself." She snapped her fingers and scolded herself before Zilla could make a fool of her. "And Florence Barbour. Of course, I forgot her talent. She can double herself."

"And triple and whatever the word for fourthing and fifthing is," Zilla said. "Extremely handy. The only real problem is activating it accidentally. If she slips and falls, suddenly we have an extra Florence to deal with."

"What happens to the duplicates when you no longer require their assistance?"

One of the Florences had come to greet them and overheard the question. "We only last seven or nine hours, depending on how much we exert ourselves. Obviously with all the work here, we've been going through us every five hours or so."

Trafalgar said, "You're... aware that you're a duplicate?"

"Of course," the Florence said, smiling with confusion. "Might get a little complicated if we all thought we were the real deal, aye?"

"I suppose."

The Florence led them back up the way she'd come. "Maybe it would help if I explain it a little. We don't see ourselves as duplicates. We're extensions of her. Imagine if you could peel off one of your arms and let it do your laundry while your other arm is cooking dinner, and your head is reading a novel. When our time is up, we go back to Florence and she takes us back in with a full memory of everything we did while we were away."

"That sounds amazing."

"It is!" Another Florence added, wiping the sweat from her brow. "We burn a lot of energy. Eat more than our share, sleep as much as possible... Sleep is the one thing we can't do for the main Florence, unfortunately."

"But we can keep working while she sleeps," a third Florence interjected, "and we pull ten times the weight of everyone else. So we're granted a little leeway."

Trafalgar shook her head. "Must get confusing."

Zilla shrugged. "I thought so at first, but I just treat them all like Flo. Sadie's the one who vexes me the most. Fuckin' sprite can run circles around us and most of the time does it just to show off. Between the food she eats and keeping Florence full of energy for splitting up, there's hardly enough food left for me 'n' Vi at the end of the day." She looked at Trafalgar, suddenly realizing something. "I hope you made your own arrangements for meals."

Trafalgar smiled. "Yes, I'll be quite well left to my own devices."

One of the Florences approached with a tall blonde woman. She was on the older side as far as Elephants went, in her mid-thirties, and wore a shirt which looked like it had been rescued from a rag bin. Her torn and muddy trousers were held up by a pair of thick suspenders. A few curls had fallen free from the sloppy pinning and hung loose around a warm, freckled face. She nodded hello, smiling warmly as she checked her dirty palm and opted not to offer it in greeting.

"Miz Trafalgar. Violet Rhys. Proud to make your acquaintance." A soft but clear Welsh accent smoothed the edge of every word, and her eyes shone with excitement. "Glad we're meetin' now, 'stead of when we were enemies. I would have taken an issue with that, to be sure."

"Yes, it is quite fortunate."

Violet shifted uncomfortably, looking like she both wanted to flee and also to remain where she was for as long as possible. "I-I've followed your career for some time. I would scour the papers for word of your adventures, wishing I could be there for one of them. Now here I am! Can hardly believe it."

Trafalgar was flummoxed, but managed a sincere smile. "Why thank you, Violet."

Zilla had been watching their exchange with an unreadable expression. When it was clear Violet was done, she smirked and coughed into her hand. "I was going to escort Trafalgar to where we've been staying, but perhaps you would like the honor instead, Violet."

Violet's eyes widened before she shrunk back against herself. "Oh, I should probably stay..."

"I insist," Zilla said. "It will save us from spending the next hour hearing you fawn about finally meeting the indomitable Miss Trafalgar."

She and the nearby Florence chuckled, and Violet blushed deep red. "Well, if she doesn't object..."

"I would be delighted to have a chance to get to know you better, Violet Rhys." She looked around the site. "My only qualm is that I wasn't able to meet Sadie Halladay..."

Zilla looked around. "She's probably around here somewhere. She'll slow down in a bit. Trust me, a little of her goes a long way." Her hat flipped up as her head suddenly rocked to one side. She shouted, "I knew you were listening in, you twit! Come say hello to our new colleague like a damn person!"

The air around them remained silent.

Zilla grunted. "Sorry. Some of us took being civilized better than others."

"That's quite all right," Trafalgar said. "We'll either learn to like one another or how to avoid each other. For now, I would much like to settle in. My journey wasn't exactly long and arduous, however..."

"Absolutely." Zilla tossed the car key to Violet. "Take as long as you need."

"You shush," Violet hissed. She ducked her chain, reached up to untie her hair, then ruffled the curls to let them fall freely. "Shall we, Miss Trafalgar?"

Trafalgar tried not to be distracted by the still-trembling blonde curls. "On one condition. You must call me Trafalgar. Enough of that 'Miss' twaddle."

Violet beamed brightly, ducked her chin, and all but skipped to the car. Trafalgar looked at Zilla, who laughed and shook her head.

"Good luck, Trafalgar."

"My thanks," she said as she followed Violet. "I feel as if I may need it."

Their accommodations were located in the nearest town. Trafalgar could smell the sea in the air even before she saw the sun glinting off the water of the river. Violet remained silent for most of the drive, quivering in her anxiousness, but pointed over the steering wheel at the stretch of blue ahead of them. "That's River Orwell," she said.

"Ah," Trafalgar said. When no further statement was forthcoming, she asked, "Is it famous?"

Violet hesitated. "No, not... no, it's just... I thought the name was pretty..."

Trafalgar couldn't resist a chuckle. "It is, indeed. Perhaps it means 'O'er Wales.' Although we're quite far away for that to be the case."

"O'er Wales," Violet said dreamily. "Oh, I quite like that. Like it a lot."

"I thought you would, Violet."

Violet glanced over, then quickly put her focus back on the road. "Vi. You can call me Vi, if you prefer. The girls tend to, and I'm used to it by now."

"I think I'll stick with Violet, if it's all the same to you. It's a lovely name. Violet is the color of powerful magic."

"Sure," Violet said. "It just saves a bit of time, is all."

Trafalgar, drawing on some of the brazenness that had rubbed off on her from associating with Dorothy Boone, said, "I don't mind spending a little extra time with you, dear."

Violet made a quiet sound of... amusement? Bashfulness? Whatever it was, she resumed her silence until they arrived at a small family home on a quiet residential street. Trafalgar had expected an inn or hotel, but she decided she shouldn't have been surprised when Leonard and Agnes footed the bill. Renting a house for the duration of their stay was absolutely in character for those two. Violet parked in a detached garage and escorted Trafalgar inside.

"We call this Wessex Base, in honor of Seaxburh. There's three bedrooms. We've pretty much all staked our claim already..."

"I've spent many lovely nights on couches," Trafalgar said, "and I'm capable of a few more. I have no interest in kicking anyone out of their beds."

Violet hesitated. "Oh, then... then that's great! Well done."

Trafalgar wondered if the girl had intended to share her room, then wondered what her response to such an offer would have been. She filed that question away for another time.

"We've got a bathroom schedule in the mornings," Violet continued. "We can work out how to add another person to the rotation later tonight. Meals are taken whenever convenient. Food is communal, so be warned about that if Florence or Sadie are around. And if you get bored, I have books you can borrow."

"Ah! I'll definitely be taking you up on that. I packed light, so I had to make some difficult choices."

"You're welcome to look over what I have. Not much of a library, but it'll do." She brushed her hands over her slacks, sighed at the smut on her palms, and clasped them behind her back. "I am sorry to have met you in such a state."

"Nonsense. Dirty hands are a sign of honest work. No one should apologize for that. If anything, it raises you in my regard."

"Lovely," Violet said, breathless again.

Trafalgar made a note to not bait the girl so much. It was fun to be idolized this way but abusing the girl's fancies would be quite rude.

"I'll, um, let you get situated, washed up... oh, washroom is just through there. Plenty of towels and soaps, whatever you need. I'll be upstairs. Just give a shout if you need anything or need a ride somewhere or... or if you need anything." Her nose wrinkled as she mentally kicked herself for such a silly repetition. "I'll leave you alone now."

"Thank you, Violet. I promise, you've been an absolute delight. I look forward to getting to know you over the course of this adventure."

Violet smiled brightly and bounced on the balls of her feet. "And it's been fantastic to finally meet you as well, M-mm..." She caught herself. "Trafalgar."

Trafalgar winked at her.

Violet headed upstairs. Trafalgar picked up her bag and carried it into the living room. She had just placed it on the couch when Violet reappeared.

"Oh, almost forgot my manners. In case Zilla didn't already say it, welcome to Suffolk."

"Thank you, Violet. I have a feeling we're going to have a grand time together."

## CHAPTER FOUR

DOROTHY WAS expecting her guest to arrive in a singular manner, but she was still caught off-guard when the light coming through the parlor windows darkened in an instant and the temperature in the house dropped several degrees. She saw her breath pluming out of her mouth as she put down her book and rose from the armchair. She moved to check the front steps but caught herself when she saw the person standing in the foyer despite no sound of the door being opened.

The woman's overcoat was so long that it pooled around her feet, which gave the impression that a pillar of oil had risen from the hardwood. The coat seemed to absorb light, more than simple black velvet. Looking at it hurt Dorothy's eyes but she forced herself to keep her face forward as she approached. The woman's face was veiled by thin lace that prevented her features from being clearly seen. The house was dark as midnight now, though she could still see light seeping in around the curtains.

"The Dov, I assume," Dorothy said, pronouncing it 'dah-v' as she'd been told it was pronounced.

"You are Lady Dorothy Boone, the woman who assigned herself a title of nobility despite having no such claim."

Dorothy said, "In a world where certain individuals require a reason to respect you, it helps to ease their way with a title. You'd know something about that, wouldn't you, Dov? I doubt you would be quite so feared under the name Renata Koessel."

The Dov made a sound that could have been a sigh or a laugh, but Dorothy couldn't see enough of her face to make a judgment.

"When you summoned me, you~"

"Oh, come off it," Dorothy snapped. "I've lived with Beatrice Sek enough to know empty showmanship when I see it. None of this is necessary. I know how powerful you are without the smoke and mirrors. And I didn't summon you, I requested your expertise. You're not a spirit, you're a woman with a vast amount of power. I may lack your supernatural abilities, but I have quite a bit of power of my own. Kindly do me the favor of treating me like an equal."

The darkness remained for a moment longer, then dispelled as quickly as it had descended. The Dov removed her veil and folded it into one of the pockets of her cloak. Dorothy smiled and dipped her head in greeting.

"Thank you for agreeing to come to me. The situation is quite unusual."

"I've heard whispers. She's upstairs?"

Dorothy nodded. "I'll show you the way."

She felt completely revitalized. The conversation with Trafalgar about sending Beatrice to some facility had finally spurred her back to work. She would no longer sit and sulk, wasting time watching a pot which may never boil. Action had to be taken, and who better to save their friend? Dorothy had solved impossible problems before and she wouldn't let her emotional investment stop her from solving this one.

She had almost reached the second floor when she realized the Dov wasn't following her. She turned to see the witch had stopped on the first floor landing. She stood perfectly still save for her eyes, which were sweeping the walls as if appraising the pattern on them.

"Is something wrong?"

"She's here."

"Beatrice? She's actually in my bedroom..."

The Dov held out one hand, palm down. "She's here. Passing through here. I met Bao Tai Sek once, four years ago. When I'm in the presence of someone that powerful, I make a point of remembering their energy. Everyone takes up space in the firmament, and everyone leaves ripples. Powerful people like her leave an unmistakable imprint when they pass."

Dorothy came back down to stand beside the Dov. She listened but couldn't hear anything.

"You can sense when a house is empty," the Dov said. "Think about moments when you feel someone behind you and turn, but no one is there."

"I suppose. Beatrice? Are you... here?"

The Dov raised both hands, closed her eyes, and ducked her chin. The air suddenly seemed thicker, as if they had sunken deeper into a pool of water and the pressure increased. Dorothy breathed in deeply and put a hand against her chest.

"Dorothy?"

She looked at the Dov, but her eyes had changed. They were darker and... familiar. Dorothy cupped the stranger's face.

"Trix?"

A wary smile. "I think so. I'm always here, but it's never now. Or it's never... any time. It's difficult to explain and my head is... this woman's head is pounding." She winced. "I believe I shouldn't stay very long, for her sake." She grabbed Dorothy's hand, squeezed it tightly. "Leave me be, Dorothy."

"What?" Dorothy put her other hand on top of Beatrice's. "You know I can't."

"And *you* know you can't do anything to help me sitting in a room staring at my face. I know what you've sacrificed for me. I know the hours you've stood watch. But it's enough."

Dorothy blinked back tears. "I love you."

"Of course I know that, my heart," Beatrice said. "And I love you. And that's why I'm letting you go. Live your life. Give me time to heal."

"So you are healing?"

Beatrice hesitated. "I... I can't swear to that. Something is happening to me, I can tell that much is true. But I don't know what it is. All I know is that the world needs you more than I do right now."

Dorothy touched the face she now saw as Beatrice. She didn't know if it was magic or some mental trickery she was doing to herself, but the features were unmistakable.

"I will find you. Whatever it takes." She looked at Beatrice's lips. "If I were to kiss you, would I be kissing you, or~"

Beatrice solved the problem by kissing Dorothy. Dorothy clung to her, eyes squeezed closed and her hands clutching the dark material of the Dov's cloak. There was no question in her mind who she was kissing, having kissed Beatrice enough times, and she was equally certain when she was kissing someone else. She stepped back and turned her head away, but kept her eyes closed so she wouldn't see the truth before it was absolutely necessary.

"You have my apologies."

"None are required," the Dov said, lightly touching her lips. "It's not my first possession. These things happen. I'm still willing to examine Beatrice, just to see if there's anything I can do for the poor dear."

"Of course," Dorothy said. "I'll take you up."

The Dov seemed unconcerned by the intimate moment they'd just shared. Dorothy was shaken by the brief glimpse of her love, their first conversation in months. To see her, touch her, hear her voice again... she knew none of that was really true. But if it had been her spirit, then did it matter whose body she was wearing?

Once they were in the room, Dorothy remained by the door. The Dov stood beside the bed and reached down to place her hand on Beatrice's forehead and closed her eyes. She nodded as if this contact was enough to confirm her diagnosis.

"She used too much magic. I asked..." Dorothy's voice failed her and she looked at the curtains until she trusted herself to continue. "I asked her to defend our home. I asked her to fight. She used too much."

"To focus that much magic, her tattoo must have been burning like an ember."

"She never said anything..."

"Exactly," the Dov said. "Because you would have told her to stop if you knew she was nearing her limits. She said nothing."

Dorothy said, "I still asked her to do it."

The Dov said, "Go downstairs, Lady Boone, and bring me a car."

"What?"

"Find a car, any car will do, and bring it up to me. Piece by piece if you must, but I simply must have a car in this room right now."

Dorothy stared at her in disbelief. "You're mad."

The Dov's eyebrows lifted. "You won't do it?"

"Of course not! Unless..." She looked at the woman in the bed. "Will... will it help her...?"

The Dov said, "No. And you refused the request because you know your limitations, just as Bao Tai Sek knows her own. You made the request. She made the choice. If you simply must feel guilt, you have made one terrible error. She is the Earth elemental, which means she draws energy from the ground. Dirt, trees, plants, stone. And you have placed her in the highest room of your house, as far from any of that as possible."

Dorothy sighed and straightened her shirt cuffs. "Can anything be done?"

The Dov clicked her tongue and continued drawing symbols in the bed above Beatrice's body. "Yes, I believe so. You will not approve of how it sounds, but I assure you it will be of the most benefit to her long-term health."

"Anything."

"We must bury her."

Dorothy's eyes widened. "Out of the question!"

The Dov glared. "Then you will bury her permanently. She needs to be recharged. She has been drained more than anyone should be, and it's only because she started out with extraordinary strength that she's still alive. Her physical body lacks the power to wake up, so her spirit wanders this house. When she gets her power back, the soul will return and she will wake."

"So I should go downstairs and begin digging a hole?"

"No. I will take her somewhere safe, somewhere nearby. The ground there is enchanted, and it will heal her faster than ordinary soil. It will still take time, of course, but it will be the best place for her to get back what's been lost."

Dorothy looked at Beatrice and remembered what she'd said. Tears pricked at her eyes, but she nodded. "Do whatever you need. Just help her."

"I'll do absolutely everything in my power. I swear it. I must call some of my associates so we can move her. Is there a telephone?"

"In my office." The Dov started to leave, but Dorothy stopped her. "There's something else. Recently, Trafalgar and I were approached by a… by a person with information pertaining to future events. This person insisted that we must do everything in our power to stop the spread of magic in the world. The Great War opened a door that she believed must remain closed. For reasons that I'm sure are obvious to you, Trafalgar and I have both come to agree with her. Humanity must end its reliance on magic if we're to survive. What do you make of that?"

The Dov considered the question. "Why would you want to prevent people from using magic?"

"That much power in the wrong hands could be devastating. And we have been warned that the time will come when too many people have used too much magic, and it simply… goes away. And we're standing here looking at proof that a sudden loss of magic could prove fatal to people who rely on it."

"You would stop people from using magic despite knowing how much good it can do in the world? Despite the fact your friend is one of the most powerful practitioners I've ever seen?"

Dorothy rolled her eyes. "Oh, I know it's a fool's errand to stop magic use entirely. People like you and Beatrice would still be able to access it, I'm sure. But you've seen the world in the past decade. Armies conjuring storms, wars fought by conjurers, strange creatures rising from the depths. Magic is flooding this world and if we don't attempt to build a dam, it will drown us."

The Dov considered Dorothy's argument. Then she said, "Cars."

"Pardon? Is this another hypothetical about automobiles?"

"Yes. It wasn't that long ago that everyone was content to go around on foot or by carriage. Then the motorcar appeared, and the world was changed in the blink of an eye. Blasted things rumble and grumble all over London at all hours of the night. People die in collisions, or get run over by them. But they make life easier. Everything is more convenient now. Distance means little now that it can be crossed as quickly as a finger snap. Cars are a convenience and a menace, Lady Boone, but people would not take lightly to someone who tried to take them away. If you and Trafalgar truly intend to make this your mission, then I will only offer you a warning: you will have a war on your hands, and the soldiers you fight will be armed with weapons you can't even begin to fathom."

Dorothy nodded sagely. "I'll keep that in mind."

"See that you do." She looked back at Beatrice once more. "In the office, you said...?"

"Yes."

The Dov left, and Dorothy went to sit on the foot of the bed, watching Beatrice and hoping she hadn't doomed the woman she loved.

## CHAPTER FIVE

IN SUFFOLK, at the same time Dorothy was entertaining a witch, Trafalgar had just begun a new day with the Keepings' group of reformed Elephants. Her first night at Wessex Base had required quite a bit of adjustment and compromise. She was accustomed to cramped quarters due to cohabitating with Dorothy and Beatrice, but Threadneedle was a palace compared to the rental. There were perks to her new houseguests, such as Florence using one of her proxies to cook everyone breakfast while the main Florence bathed upstairs.

Trafalgar was at the breakfast table with her tea, looking over a book of notes Sadie had provided, when Violet came down. She was barefoot, still in her dressing gown, with her hair pinned up for bed. She cut across the doorway of the dining room and went directly to the kitchen.

"Flo," she said, voice hushed and breathless, "I need some of your perfume."

"For the dig? Who're you trying to impress? You think the queen will turn us away if we're a bit sweaty?"

Violet said, "Don't be daft. I just... I want to smell nice."

"Little stink has never bothered any of us before."

"I looked like a drowned rat when Trafalgar showed up yesterday! I want–"

There was a sharp hissing sound, followed by a quick whispering back and forth. Trafalgar brought her teacup to her mouth, knowing it did nothing to conceal her amused expression. Violet poked her head around the door frame. She disappeared. Then she strolled casually into view. She tugged at her nightgown, fingers curled against her palms. She smiled but refused to look directly at Trafalgar.

"Good morning, Trafalgar," she said, meek.

"Pardon?" Trafalgar said.

"Good morning, is all."

Trafalgar said, "Good morning, Violet. I was off in my own mind, thinking about the day ahead of us. I didn't even realize you'd come down."

Violet looked skeptical. "I only came down to, ah, to ask Flo a quick question. I still need to wash up and finish getting dressed. Obviously." She laughed nervously. "Well, now this is twice that I've appeared in front of you looking like absolute shambles. Whatever must you think of me."

"We all need time to fully wake up, don't we." Trafalgar took a point to hold the pause before she added, "But for the record, you look like a dream."

Violet blushed, revealing freckles. "Save me some eggs?"

Trafalgar gestured an acknowledgement with her teacup. "As you wish."

Violet turned and fled upstairs.

Trafalgar let out the chuckle she'd been holding in and looked back at the notes. Sadie's speed made her the perfect candidate for taking notes about the dig, but her handwriting left much to be desired. The ink was smeared, the letters horribly slanted, and occasionally entire sentences blurred together into a single word. It was a strain on her eyes when she first started reading, but now she felt she'd discovered the rhythm. She found the spot where she'd left off and continued.

Over the past few decades, the owners of the property had found evidence that it was used as a ritualistic burial site. The area was full of grassy mounds, like waves frozen in time, and a handful of these had been pillaged by grave robbers and treasure hunters. While they made off with some trinkets, their thievery proved there was something under the ground worth digging for.

The Keepings' focus was on the largest swell of land on the north side of the property. Agnes was absolutely certain it was a burial-ship. Trafalgar had never heard of such a thing. The body of a great and beloved leader was placed in a ship with various grave goods - weapons, coins, gold, and the like - and the entire thing was buried. She imagined this, like a pharaoh's tomb, would allowed the deceased to arrive in the afterlife in a manner befitting their earthly status.

She knew how much work was involved to bury an ordinary coffin; burying an entire boat must have been an absolutely grueling task.

So far, the Keepings' team had found proof that there was definitely a ship buried under the mound. They had found rivets, nails, and fossilized bits of wood. They were proceeding with the utmost caution to prevent damage to the artifacts. This morning they would finally breach the interior hull of the ship, which was the reason Trafalgar had been summoned.

It was time to look inside the tomb.

She had put aside the notes to eat breakfast by the time Violet returned. She was dressed for the excavation in a light brown shirt, neckerchief, and flared pants. Trafalgar couldn't help but detect a scent of perfume as Violet took the seat next to her with a plate of breakfast. She took a bite before risking a look to her left.

"A proper good morning to you, Trafalgar."

"And to you, Violet. You look lovely this morning."

Violent smiled and gestured at the book. "Getting all caught up?"

"Mm, yes. It seems as if you've done all the hard work and I'll be swooping in to take the glory."

A Florence, but not the one who had cooked breakfast, joined them. "It's the way it ought to be," she said. "We've all been working so hard on this, we have a bias. We need it to be something. You can judge it properly."

Violet said, "You and Lady Boone have a reputation. You won't pretend it was all your doing, if it does turn out to be something. You'll make sure credit is given where it's due."

"I knew we had a reputation," Trafalgar said, and checked the time. "That is much nicer than the one I thought we had. Are Zilla and Sadie going to be joining us?"

"Zilla is upstairs getting ready," Florence said. "She never eats breakfast. And Sadie is already at the site. She leaves around dawn, chooses to run instead of riding with us."

Violet shrugged and swallowed a bit of egg. "Like we've said, she's not the most social. She liked being a pickpocket. She was really good at it for obvious reasons. When we decided to go straight~"

Florence said, "Well, it was mostly decided for us..."

"Right," Violet agreed. "Work with the Mnemosyne Society or go to prison. Not much of a choice there. But she stayed because she likes some of us. A few of us. Some days, anyway. But if she had her way, she'd have just gone solo and kept thieving."

Trafalgar examined Violet's face. "Why did *you* choose to stay?"

Violet shrugged and idly turned her teacup in a circle on the tabletop, using her fingertips to spin it clockwise on the saucer.

"Like I said, not much of a choice... but I like the Keepings. They seem like good folks." She seemed content to leave it at that, then looked up at Trafalgar and just as quickly looked elsewhere. "And you. You're... famous. I wanted to be on the same team as someone like you for a change."

Trafalgar smiled. "If I may ask, what led you to Maud Keaton in the first place?"

Violet started to answer, but Florence cleared her throat in a pointed manner. "There will be time for that later. For now, we should get a shake on. We don't want to waste a moment of sunlight."

"Ah, very true." Trafalgar gathered her plate as well as Violet's. "We should definitely continue this conversation another time. Perhaps when this matter is settled and we've returned to London."

Violet puffed up, her chest and shoulders rising as she tried to contain her joy. "I think that would be quite nice, Trafalgar."

Florence snorted quietly but said nothing as Trafalgar took the plates into the kitchen. She heard the women she'd left behind whispering but pretended she couldn't. She scraped the remnants into the compost and cleaned the plates in the basin, thinking about Violet. It was lovely to be flirted with, flattering and quite a boost to her ego, but something about it felt forbidden. She was with Dorothy and Beatrice. Wasn't she? Dorothy hadn't shared her bed since Beatrice fell, so part of her felt as if their relationship was stalled, if not over entirely. They wouldn't be together while Beatrice was in her current condition, so were they finished? Was she unattached?

Zilla came into the kitchen as Trafalgar finished with the dishes. "Big day ahead of us."

Trafalgar nodded.

Zilla came closer and put a hand on Trafalgar's shoulder. She could feel something sharp against the material, one of the paralyzing spines that had proven her undoing at their last dust-up. Trafalgar tensed and looked at Zilla, who was staring straight ahead through the window as if checking the weather. When she spoke, her voice was low and her lips barely moved.

"That girl is older than all of us, 'cept maybe for you, but her heart is about as young as it can be. If you're cruel to her, I'll be real cruel to you in equal measure."

"I have no intention of cruelty," Trafalgar promised, equally hushed. "But I'll keep your warning at the front of my mind for all future interactions."

"See that you do." Zilla lifted her hand, shot the spike into the sink, and plucked it up. "I just wanted to be crystal clear we were on the same page."

Trafalgar nodded. "It's good to see your loyalty to each other is as strong as it was when you called yourselves Elephants."

Zilla said, "Maud Keaton was just someone who gave us a place to belong. The Keepings are just people who give us purpose. The person in charge might change, but we always stay the same. We look out for each other no matter what."

"It's admirable."

"Nah," Zilla said. "It's the only way some of us can stay alive. We're leaving in five minutes. Be in the car or walk to the site."

Trafalgar said, "I'll be ready."

Zilla nodded and left the kitchen. Trafalgar watched her go, waiting until she was alone before she smiled. She'd been skeptical about reforming the women, but she foolishly hadn't counted on the bond between them being stronger than blind obedience to their leader. It didn't matter if they were thieves or archaeologists or whatever Cecil Dubourne was doing with his group. The talented members of the Forty Elephants were, and always had been, women above all else.

And women, at the end of the day, looked out for one another.

They were ready to breach the ship by mid-afternoon. A trio of Florences made the final push, breaking through the topsoil to reveal a wooden hatch in the side of the ship. It seemed very convenient to Trafalgar that they'd known to dig at the exact spot where they'd find an entrance, but Violet smiled proudly and pointed her forefinger and pinkie at her eyes. "I took a peek, knew where to dig."

"Faraway eyes," Trafalgar said.

"Just so," Violet said.

Sadie dug out the ship's interior at blinding speed. Trafalgar wanted to voice a warning that she should be careful, but Zilla stopped her before she had even finished the sentence.

"It looks rushed and sloppy to us, but she's explained it before. She's taking hours to do this work. She's meticulous, while we're standing here like statues."

There was a sudden shudder in the air, and a woman appeared in front of Trafalgar. She wore a man's undershirt and her exposed arms, shoulders, and face were as filthy as if she had erupted out of the topsoil like a mole. She was dripping sweat and completely breathless, her short hair standing up in spikes as she made a grabbing motion at Zilla, who retrieved a canteen and handed it over. The woman pressed her lips to the mouth, tilted her head back, and swallowed half of it in a single go.

Trafalgar looked past her and saw the piles of dirt near the burial site had doubled in size. "How..."

"She's quick," Zilla said.

Sadie Halladay finished the canteen and wiped her hand across her mouth. "I'm quick," she panted.

Trafalgar looked at her, impressed. "We haven't been properly—"

"Yeah, I know who you are."

With another gust, the woman vanished. Trafalgar watched the mounds of excavated dirt and actually saw one of them grow.

Zilla chuckled. "You might not have met her, but you've been part of her scenery for... oh..." She narrowed her eyes and tried to calculate. "You got here about twenty-nine hours ago... I'd say that's about a year in her time."

"You can't be serious. She doesn't look a day over twenty."

"She doesn't age when she's spriting," Zilla said. "Maud once said she runs faster than time can find her, which is as good an explanation as any. To be honest, most of us stopped looking for reason behind our curses a long time ago."

Trafalgar said, "You think they're a curse?"

"Some call it a curse, some call it gifts. It's made all of us different, and that's rarely a good thing in this world."

"True..."

They were interrupted by Sadie's return. "I've gotten most of it cleared out. There really wasn't much to dig through. The deck and hull were mostly intact, so it kept out a lot more than we thought. Vi's been checking things out all morning and she seems confident everything is stable. If you're ready to go in, I'd say now's as good a time as any."

"Wonderful!" She clapped her hands together and looked past Sadie to see Violet standing near the hatch. "I should probably take someone in with me to confirm my findings. Just to prevent any accusations of improper procedure in the future."

Zilla said, "What an idea, and I wonder who you might be thinking about..."

Trafalgar didn't bother trying to lie. She called out to Violet and waved her over.

Fifteen minutes later, they were outfitted in heavy coats, gloves, and protective headgear that looked like a pie-tin turned upside down. The outfit was just a precaution in case their excavation had disturbed the ship's integrity and caused the deck to collapse. Zilla also provided a pair of goggles which enhanced the ambient light by twenty percent, which would bolster the beam of their torches considerably.

Trafalgar was fitted into a harness which would be lowered through the hatch. Zilla and a few Florences would monitor from the surface. She looked across the opening and saw Violet, adorable in her tin hat, goggles, and too-big coat. She offered a wink, and Violet smiled.

"Is this your first tomb?" Trafalgar asked.

"Yes, actually. Anything I should know?"

"Don't rub any lamps." She grinned.

Trafalgar sat on the edge of the hatch. She checked once more to ensure Zilla and the duplicates were in place, then slipped over into the hole and let the rope take her weight. She was carefully lowered into the darkness, the fresh sea air immediately replaced with a stale, musty stench. She let go of the rope just long enough to tug the kerchief up over her mouth and nose.

Zilla lowered her slowly enough that she could make out the far end of the space, and she approximated the ship was twenty meters from stem to stern. Her torchlight swept across support beams and oarlocks, though any benches for the sailors who used them had been removed. A platform took up the central position of the space, and she could already see it was surrounded by regalia: weapons, coins, crowns, jewels, and the like.

"I can already see this is quite a find!" she called to the women above. A cynical part of her brain also made a note to check Sadie's supplies to ensure she hadn't slipped away with anything.

Her feet touched solid ground and she tugged on the rope. It went slack enough that she could remove the harness and stepped to one side so it could be pulled back up for Violet. Trafalgar stood in one spot and slowly moved her light across everything in her line of sight. The trinkets twinkled, while the ancient wood had been reclaimed by the earth and seemed to absorb the light.

Violet arrived from above in a mask similar to Trafalgar's. Her eyes were comically wide behind the lenses of her goggles. She stared at the platform ahead of them.

"Is that actually... a queen? Who has been at rest here for over a thousand years?"

"There's only one way to be certain," Trafalgar said.

They approached carefully. The wood flooring had rotted enough that she could feel it straining at every step, sagging beneath her boots no matter how carefully she placed them. She had almost reached what she dubbed the crypt when something snapped under Violet's foot. One hand shot out and she grabbed hold of Trafalgar's arm, but the plank had only snapped across its width. The soil beneath was solid enough that she was in no danger of actually falling or sinking.

"That scared the life out of me," she gasped.

"Me as well." Trafalgar looked down at the hand still clutching her bicep. "Are you all right?"

"Just shaken up." She followed Trafalgar's gaze. "Oh. I'm sorry."

Trafalgar shook her head. "No apologies necessary. You may hold onto my arm if it makes you feel safer."

Violet moved her hand to Trafalgar's shoulder. They moved together toward the crypt, and Trafalgar held her torch so it would illuminate the surface. Violet moved closer and twisted her head to read the inscriptions.

"Can you read that?"

"No. Dorothy would be able to tell if it identified Seaxburh. We should take rubbings."

Violet said, "Sadie can run them down to London for us."

Trafalgar nodded. She had expected dust, but the biggest problem here was mud and mold. "We were fortunate the upper deck hasn't collapsed. The weight of the soil could have crushed this and destroyed any hope of identifying who this might be."

"The crown and scepter indicate a ruler," Violet said. "And no commoner would be laid to rest with a treasure like this."

"We should take a closer look at some of these relics. It's unthinkable that a queen would be left in an unmarked grave, even if her reign was controversial."

Violet said, "Can we just wait a moment? Can we stand here? No one has stood here in hundreds and hundreds of years, and the last people who did may have been burying their queen. One of the first queens in history. I just want to be sure I remember that."

Trafalgar smiled and touched Violet's hand. "I do, too."

"I'm... mm."

"What?"

Violet lowered her voice, preventing an echo. "There are other rumors about you and Lady Boone. They would prevent me from saying what I was about to say."

Trafalgar considered that. "Well, whatever truth may be in those rumors, I don't think it would prevent you from speaking your mind."

Violet still hesitated. Then finally she said, "I never thought I would be doing something this amazing. This discovery could change the way the world sees the past. And I get to be here for it! I'm grateful for that. And I'm very grateful to be sharing this moment with you."

They looked at each other, the emotion of the moment only slightly tempered by the goggles and clothes over the lower part of their faces.

"Viol~"

"Good lord," Violet said, cutting Trafalgar off, her eye drawn to something near the stern.

Trafalgar turned and saw a woman standing in the beam of light cast by the open hatch. She was shorter than both of them, dressed in chain mail over a long flowing tunic. Her red hair was center-parted, and she wore a jeweled circlet that shined more than could be explained with the available light. Her hands rested on the hasp of a sword with its blade planted in the ground at her feet.

"Invaders," she intoned.

"What does that mean?" Violet asked. "That we're intruding on her final resting place?"

Trafalgar said, "No, she said invaders... oh, crumbs." She looked at Violet. "You weren't born in England, were you?"

"Ebbw Vale."

"I'll take that as a no." Trafalgar faced the woman again. "My lady, we meant no disrespect~"

"*Invaders*, your trespass shall not go unpunished. Leave this place at once and return to your own lands!"

She lifted the sword and slammed it into the ground. It impacted with a sound like thunder, and a tidal wave crashed through the wall behind her, shattering the decrepit wood with an impossible amount of force. Trafalgar pivoted on the ball of her feet and wrapped her arms around Violet as the wave flooded through the chamber and slammed into them.

## CHAPTER SIX

TRAFALGAR COUGHED up a mouthful of water. Strong hands rolled her onto her side as she coughed again, producing another flood that crashed down onto a floor. Someone was speaking, but her mind was still trying to catch up with her body and couldn't focus on the words. She was in a bed, she was in a house. She was dry. She was still coughing, but the water wasn't coming out anymore. Someone's hand cupped the back of her head, and someone else squeezed her hand.

When the coughing finally stopped, she fell flat onto her back and stared up at the same ceiling she'd seen when she woke that morning. Her chest felt as if someone had just been standing on her sternum with a heavy boot. She looked up at a circle of concerned faces: most of them Florence, but Sadie and Zilla were also there. Zilla muttered something to one of the Florences, who hurried from the room.

"Violet?" she rasped.

"She's here," Zilla said. "She was in the same state as you. Hasn't woken up yet."

The Florence who had left came back. Dorothy Boone was right behind her, and Trafalgar had rarely been so relieved to see her.

"So this is what it takes to get you out of the house these days," Trafalgar said.

Dorothy's face flinched in an attempt to smile, but it was a pathetic failure. She bent over the bed to check Trafalgar's eyes.

"How do you feel? What do you remember?"

"Seaxburh. We saw a... remnant of her, perhaps a spirit." It hurt to speak, due to the breathing required, and her throat ached. "Was anyone else hurt? In the flood?"

Dorothy looked at Zilla, who was the one that answered. "There wasn't a flood, not that any of us saw. We waited for you to call back up to us, but you never did. Sadie finally zipped down and saw you and Violet sprawled on the floor unconscious, both of you sopping wet. We managed to get you back up to the surface, but weren't able to wake you."

Trafalgar suddenly realized Dorothy's presence, combined with the quality of light coming in through the window, meant it couldn't be the same day they'd gone into the tomb.

"How long were we unconscious?"

A Florence looked at the clock and blinked in surprise. "Cor blimey," she whispered. "I figure it was twenty-four hours exactly. We don't know exactly when you was knocked out, a'course, but yeah seems about right. How about that?"

Before anyone could respond, Violet began coughing across the room. Everyone turned toward in that direction except for Dorothy, but Trafalgar waved her off.

"See that she's okay."

There was the splash of water again; the floor of the room must have been completely underwater. Violet coughed longer and rougher than Trafalgar had, but finally she was able to croak a single word: "Trafalgar?"

"She's here," Zilla said, looking over her shoulder. "She just woke up, too. You both had us pretty scared. No, lie down, we'll take care of whatever you need."

They went over the story again, and Trafalgar tuned them out, rubbing the bridge of her nose. She ached all over, but especially in her chest, throat, and just behind her eyes. They must have triggered something in the tomb, some magical security measure left to protect their queen from being desecrated by her enemies. It made sense if she was as controversial as Agnes Keeping suggested. Foolish of them, in that case, to allow someone born in Ethiopia and someone else born in Wales to be the first to step inside. Of course the security measures saw them as invaders.

"Well done, Seaxburh," she said under her breath.

Zilla looked at her again. "We came to the same conclusion, basically. Agnes... oh, she's downstairs, too. Came up with Dorothy. She's going through all of her notes looking for something she might have missed about a security measure at the site, but since none of them even mentioned the site in the first place..."

Trafalgar shook her head. "We were the foolish ones. Of course they would have countermeasures." She pushed herself up. "I assume you've been monitoring us for any lingering effects?"

"Other than the unconsciousness," Florence said, "you both seem perfectly fine. And then you woke up and spilled a few liters of water on the floor. Lord... whoever Agnes rented from is going to be very cross indeed..."

Dorothy sat on the edge of Trafalgar's bed and took her hand. "We'll buy the blasted house if they make a fuss. The important thing is that you're both okay."

Trafalgar looked at Violet, who was bundled up in another twin bed against the opposite wall. She was pale, with dark spots under her eyes, and she was lying on her side with two of the Florences tending to her. She was looking at Trafalgar's hand, the fingers linked with Dorothy's, and the sadness in her eyes spoke volumes. She wanted to say something, but it was far too sensitive for this moment.

"Vi," she said. Violet looked up into her eyes, and Trafalgar smiled sadly. She hoped that she conveyed the depth of what she was thinking when she said, "I am very glad you are okay."

"I feel the same," Violet said, eyes watering. "Truly."

Dorothy squeezed Trafalgar's hand, too relieved to recognize what was being exchanged between the two women.

"I think you speak for all of us," she said.

Trafalgar knew that the words may have gone for everyone present, but the meaning behind them was only true for one other person.

Once it was determined neither woman was in immediate danger, one of the Florences ushered everyone out to give them both time to rest. She promised to come back in a little while with food, then pulled the curtains and shut the door behind her. Silence fell, although Trafalgar could still hear the murmur of conversation elsewhere in the house, and she stared at the ceiling as she took inventory of herself. Pain, yes. An odd weight behind her eyes that could just as likely be attributed to exhaustion or a remnant of being unconscious for so long.

"Trafalgar?" Violet asked softly.

"Yes? Is everything all right?"

"Everything is fine. I just..." Her voice trailed off. "Can I come over to you?"

Trafalgar looked across the gap between their beds and, after a moment, nodded. She shifted to the far side of the mattress as Violet pushed back the covers and got up on shaky legs.

"Careful..."

"Just two steps," Violet said. "Shouldn't be too taxing..."

She stumbled on the second step, turning her fall into a graceless tumble onto the bed. She positioned herself properly - shoulders on the pillow, knees together and slightly bent - and lay on her side. Trafalgar matched her position so they could face each other, but kept her legs straight so that her feet extended slightly off the bottom edge of the mattress.

"You threw yourself in front of me."

"Of course," Trafalgar said. "I'm taller than you."

Violet said, "That wave was huge. It filled the whole ship. It was going to hit both of us no matter what." Her eyes searched Trafalgar's face. Her voice, already a whisper, became softer. "You stepped in front of me anyway."

"I did," Trafalgar admitted.

They stared at each other in silence, but Trafalgar felt as if important information was passing between them regardless.

"Did Zilla or Florence tell you that Sadie experiences time different than us? You just got here the other day..."

"But I've been part of her life for, what was it, a year?"

Violet nodded. "Something like that." She brought her hand up and touched two fingers to Trafalgar's cheek. "I think I know how she feels."

"Violet..." Trafalgar averted her eyes. "There's... there are circumstances that must be addressed before anything... between us..."

"I understand," Violet said. "I'd be a fool if I expected you would be available. I knew something would be in the way. But I had to at least let you know how I felt."

"I'm very glad you did. I feel drawn to you in a way that I have rarely ever felt. But it would be unfair to everyone involved if I~"

Violet moved her fingers to Trafalgar's lips. "I know. But can I just lie here with you?"

"I would like that very much. Yes."

Violet put her head on Trafalgar's chest and closed her eyes, and Trafalgar stroked her hair until she fell asleep.

Night had fallen when Trafalgar woke. Violet was still asleep, so Trafalgar eased away from her and slipped out of the room. She was sore all over, but the pain was manageable enough if she moved slowly. She kept one hand on the wall as she descended the stairs, following the light and voices coming from below.

Agnes was seated at the dining room table with a collection of books open in front of her. She was transcribing something to a new notebook and sat up straighter when she saw Trafalgar on the stairs. She got to her feet and, even though Trafalgar waved her off, came around to offer her arm as support. Trafalgar accepted her help and leaned against her with a quiet 'thank you.'

"I must ask your forgiveness. In my eagerness to achieve my goals, I neglected to show the proper caution. There's nothing in what I've read about security measures, but~"

Trafalgar put her hand on top of Agnes' to stop her. "I would gladly accept your apology if I felt one was warranted. We've all been guilty of the same sin. Being overeager can afflict even the best of us. I could have insisted on waiting until we knew more, but I didn't. I bear no ill will against you, dear Agnes, and I hope you'll forgive me for creating such a wreckage of your great quest."

Agnes scoffed and rolled her eyes. "Now that is an unnecessary apology."

Dorothy came out of the parlor. "You should be in bed."

Trafalgar raised an eyebrow. "My, how the tables have turned. But unlike you, I've apparently spent too much time in bed already. I've lost an entire day to bed, and I shall like to stretch my legs a bit. Besides, there is something I must discuss with you in private."

"With me?" Dorothy said.

Agnes patted Trafalgar's elbow. "I'll leave you ladies alone."

"No, no," Trafalgar said, "you're all set up here. Dorothy, let's go outside to talk."

Dorothy nodded, curiosity written across her face as she moved to take Agnes' place. She slipped her arm around Trafalgar's and helped her through the kitchen and out into the tiny backyard. Trafalgar shuffled through the grass to a bench under a tree, and sighed with relief as she sat down. Dorothy sat beside her.

"Are you certain you're not hurt?"

"Oh, I'm quite hurt. But improved since this morning. Whatever magic was being used to protect the queen's burial site must have been enormously powerful." She put her hand on Dorothy's thigh. "Beatrice...?"

"Cora agreed to stay with her while I'm here. The woman I contacted for help... ah..." She shook her head. "We can discuss that later. What is it you wanted to talk about?"

Trafalgar looked up at the branches above them. "I adore you. And Beatrice. And the relationship we've developed is something I never could have imagined being part of. It's shown me who I am. I treasure every moment you've shared with me. But it's always been... you and Beatrice allowing me in. The love I feel for you both pales in comparison to the love you have for each other. I believe the unique arrangement we've created can work, but not when the emotions are so clearly unbalanced."

Dorothy said, "If we've ever made you feel~"

"No," Trafalgar interrupted. "Far from it. And the times we've shared have been magnificent. I suppose I've always known that it had to end at some point. I just ignored that knowledge because I was enjoying myself too much."

"Something's changed." Dorothy looked up at the second-story window. "Zilla mentioned you and the Welsh girl had grown especially close. I thought she simply meant you were friendly." She looked back at Trafalgar. "You have feelings for her?"

Trafalgar laughed softly and shook her head. "I don't have a clue. The way she looks at me. The way I feel when I look at her. It was immediate and unmistakable. But I refused to let myself explore it while I was still part of part of us." She took Dorothy's hand. Dorothy squeezed it. "I think I would like to step back from what we have to explore what is happening."

Dorothy's eyes shone in the darkness. "Oh, Trafalgar, of course." She leaned in and kissed Trafalgar's cheek, then her lips. "I didn't get a chance to see her conscious, but she seems lovely."

Trafalgar laughed again, this time louder. "She reminds me of you, a bit. I imagine any woman who strikes my fancy will remind me of you in some way or another."

"Why, thank you. That's quite a compliment."

"Are you feeling... yourself again?" Trafalgar asked. "You do look well."

Dorothy rolled her eyes. "On the inside, I'm terrified, anxious, worried. But I trust Cora, and Beatrice told me to take a step back, so I'm doing my best to heed her advice."

Trafalgar furrowed her brow. "Sorry, Beatrice told you...?"

"Oh. Yes. It's a long story involving a witch and spirits. I'll explain it all when you're less tired."

"It sounds as if we've both had quite an adventure today. These past two days, rather."

"Mm. I already miss the quiet."

Trafalgar brought Dorothy's hand to her mouth and kissed the knuckles.

"If the exploration with this young Welsh flower doesn't go the way you hoped, I want you to know that there will always be a place for you with us."

"Thank you, love."

They sat together in silence, listening to the sound of the wind in the branches overhead, and Dorothy tilted her head back to look at the stars. Trafalgar looked up as well.

"We should probably get you back inside," Dorothy finally said.

"I'll be fine for a few more minutes."

Dorothy started to protest but then closed her mouth. "Very well. A bit longer."

In the morning, though the health of both women had vastly improved overnight, it was decided that Trafalgar and Violet would be sent home to London to recuperate. They were able to come downstairs and join the others for breakfast and the only evidence of their ordeal was a slight stiffness to their movement. Dorothy noticed that Trafalgar chose to sit very close to Violet, who blushed whenever she was caught staring at her new compatriot. Agnes decided to remain in Suffolk to continue her research on the site.

"One benefit from everything that's happened," Trafalgar said, "is that I believe I have confirmed your belief that this is indeed where Seaxburh was laid to rest. It may not have gone as we expected, but my mission was accomplished."

Agnes thanked her profusely and again offered her apology. Again, Trafalgar refused.

They departed after breakfast, with a Florence driving them to the train station. Trafalgar and Violet shared a sleeping car so they could "stretch out," and Dorothy did them the courtesy of pretending to believe them. She highly doubted they'd been intimate yet, didn't think Trafalgar had even revealed their talk from the night before, but she also doubted they used both benches when they "laid down for a while" during the journey home.

Leonard was waiting to pick them up when they got to London. He took Trafalgar's hand in both of his and expressed his sincere regret that their little favor had turned into such an adventure.

"Never apologize for adventure," Trafalgar said. "Just promise you will never bore me."

"You have my word, Miss Trafalgar."

On the ride to Threadneedle in Leonard's sedan, Violet took Trafalgar's hand. "I regret that we have to part ways. I've gotten used to having you around..."

"I'm still nearby. London can be a very small city to one who is properly motivated. Are you living at the boardinghouse that the Keepings bought for the Elephants?"

"I am. I have my own room and everything. It's quite nice." She drummed her fingers nervously against her leg. "Shall I write down the address for you...?"

"I know where it is," Trafalgar said.

"O' course. Right. Yes."

Violet chuckled and shook her head, and Trafalgar touched her cheek lightly.

Leonard looked over his shoulder at them, then lifted his eyebrow in curiosity at Dorothy.

Dorothy smiled. "It was a *quite* eventful few days in Suffolk."

"So it would seem," Leonard agreed.

When they arrived at the townhouse, Leonard carried Trafalgar's bag to the door, while Violet went up the front steps with them to give Trafalgar a proper goodbye. Dorothy unlocked the door, intending to step into the hall and give them a bit of privacy.

As soon as the door opened, there was a sound like the sky being ripped apart over their heads. Leonard and Dorothy both actually ducked, half-expecting a bolt of lightning to crack across the street. Instead, a woman had appeared on the front steps. Dorothy stared at her in shock. She believed it was a remnant of the Dov's visit, perhaps another practitioner, but the woman was dressed in chain mail over a robe, and she wore the circlet of a ruler. She raised a magnificent sword.

"It's Seaxburh," Trafalgar gasped. "Dorothy, you can see her?"

"As clearly as I see you..."

The queen, her skin illuminated by an unseen source, raised her sword. She aimed the tip at Trafalgar.

"From beyond the veil of death, I strike at the heart of your empire."

Before Dorothy could react to the proclamation, Trafalgar and Violet both cried out in agony. Trafalgar dropped to her hands and knees, while only Leonard's quick thinking saved Violet from falling backward onto the street. He bundled her in his arms as her body convulsed. Trafalgar clutched the side of her head before the arm holding her up collapsed, and she fell onto the stairs.

The queen turned to look at Dorothy. "Your kingdom shall fall, and it shall be known that Seaxburh, Queen of the Gewisse, whose dominion grows even as she lies sleeping."

Another crack of thunder tore through the air, and the queen vanished. People passing on the street had frozen in place, looking at the cloudless sky and holding out their hands to feel for rain. Leonard was ashen, pressing his hand to Violet's slack face for signs of life. Dorothy knelt to see if Trafalgar had been injured in her fall.

"Lady Boone, Violet's skin is warm to the touch..."

Dorothy saw sweat on Trafalgar's brow and upper lip, confirmed she was also feverish with a quick touch to her cheek.

"What in blazes just happened?" Leonard asked.

"Mr. Keeping, I believe we just discovered the true curse of Seaxburh's tomb."

## CHAPTER SEVEN

THE THREADNEEDLE townhouse had become a house of the infirm. Trafalgar's bed was large enough to accommodate her and Violet together. Dorothy couldn't help but regret they hadn't learned that for themselves under much nicer circumstances. Cora Hyde, who had been upstairs tending to Beatrice and was drawn to the door by the commotion, helped Dorothy get them comfortable.

Once that was done, Dorothy called the Wessex Base to see if anything had happened at the site. Agnes informed them everyone was fine, and Sadie dashed out to the ship-burial and confirmed nothing had changed. She reinforced the fences and covered the hatch to prevent anyone from wandering in and causing more problems. Leonard left as quickly as possible to join his wife at the burial site to see if there was anything to be discovered there.

"Let's start with what we know," Cora said once he was gone. "You can lay out it for me, because I don't have a bloody clue what's happening."

Dorothy explained everything as calmly as she could, her gaze repeatedly wandering back to where Trafalgar and Violet were lying shoulder-to-shoulder on top of the blankets.

"Abraham knew more about death curses than any of us," Cora said with regret. "I believe he left most of his literary estate to Cecil. I can see if there's anything in the collection that might help us."

"Focus on the Roman and Anglo-Saxons," Dorothy said. "I doubt anything Egyptian will help us. Although... damn." She rubbed her face. "Get everything. I don't want to overlook potential answers because we narrowed our search too early."

Cora nodded and left to retrieve Cecil Dubourne. Dorothy was left alone for the first time since Trafalgar and Violet collapsed, and the emotion of the moment washed over her like a shroud. She put her hand against the wall to prevent herself from swaying, used her other hand to push her hair out of her face, and squeezed her eyes closed. She worked her jaw and fought the tremors in her shoulders and running down her spine.

Desmond was dead. Beatrice was in some sort of in-between state. Now Trafalgar...

"I can't lose her," she whispered. She pressed her fist against her forehead, eyes closed so tightly her tears couldn't squeeze out. "I will not lose *everyone.*"

She slammed the side of her fist into the wall and let the physical pain override her emotions. "Trix? Are you here?" She searched the room for signs of an eavesdropping spirit. "Give me a sign. Are you here, watching? Damn it... if you're here, help. Take control of my damn body if you have to. Make me a puppet and help them. There has to be something we can do!"

The room remained silent.

"All right then," she said. "I'll just have to save you both myself."

Dorothy unbuttoned her sleeves and rolled them up as she left Trafalgar's room and went to the office. She had countless artifacts and relics in her vault. One of them had to be useful in this situation. A summoning spell, or a healing elixir, or some sort of protective item that could reverse whatever Seaxburh had done. Perhaps she could use the spell to transfer illness from one person to another, but she believed that was only for physical ailments. She would have to be careful; using a magical cure against a magical illness could have unintended consequences, and she wasn't willing to risk making the situation worse.

She pulled out her records and placed them on the desk, flipped it open, and took a seat as she skimmed each entry for anything that looked promising.

She was still there an indeterminate amount of time later when Cora returned. She paused in the doorway of the office before coming inside.

"The Vault?" Cora asked.

"I'm thinking of changing its name, given how bloody useless it's turning out to be. What good is a protection spell or a defensive charm if it only works before you're hurt?"

Cora winced. "I'm afraid my news is only bad and worse."

"Cecil?"

"Abraham's library focused almost entirely on Egyptian death curses. He hasn't done an exhaustive study of what they say, but there's nothing about lifting them or reversing their effects."

"Oh, come on. There has to be something."

"Not in the records we have available. The curses are recorded, as are their effects, but we can find no evidence of anyone successfully thwarting one."

Dorothy pinched the bridge of her nose. "Well, perhaps the Romans were more willing to give their victims a chance to redeem themselves."

"There's always a chance." Cora's voice was gentle. "Everything you and Trafalgar have accomplished over the years, surely this will just be another adventure you regale us with over drinks at the Inkwell."

"I haven't the foggiest idea where to even begin."

Cora said, "Clearly the queen herself. You all saw her in the foyer, and even I heard her proclamation from upstairs. That is no ordinary death curse."

"Trafalgar and Violet both reported seeing her in the ship before a wall of water crashed over them. Perhaps the water was a manifestation of the curse striking them down. It only took full effect here because it sensed we were in London. The 'heart' of our empire, as it were. So the curse is somehow aware enough to know the women in the tomb weren't born on British soil and when they were back in the capital city."

"But not aware enough to know their loyalty was to Britain."

"It doesn't make sense. That much power, it would leave a mark..." Dorothy pressed two fingers to her temple and rubbed. "Perhaps it doesn't matter. At the time of her rule, England was divided into several kingdoms. It's very likely that Seaxburh would consider Londinium part of a rival territory."

"But why wait until Trafalgar is here to strike? You said she was healthy and recovering when she was still in Suffolk."

Cecil chose that moment to burst into the room. "We have a problem."

Dorothy nearly scolded him for entering her home without being invited, but she could see the pallor of the man's face and knew there were bigger issues at hand. "What's happened now?"

To Cora, he said, "You told me you were looking into Egyptian death curses?"

"Death curses in general," Cora corrected. "Did you find something pertinent in Abraham's books?"

"No. After you left, I received a call from a colleague who works at St Leonard's Hospital. It seems as if in the past hour they've received half a dozen patients with stomach cramps, fever, and various aches and pains. The symptoms all appeared out of the blue at approximately the same time. He knows I'm a member of the Mnemosyne Society and wanted to know if we were aware of anything queer happening in the city."

Dorothy said, "We have to assume this is somehow tied to what happened with Trafalgar and Violet."

"That would be a solid assumption," Cecil said, "given that all six of the patients worked here on Threadneedle Street."

Dorothy paled. "Crumbs. That's why the curse waited until they were in London before striking them down. It was a timed explosion, intended to do the maximum amount of damage."

"Let the soldiers return home with a bomb in their pocket, you might catch their leader in the explosion."

"If that's true, those six will only be the first of many." She pressed two fingers to her temple and looked down at the desk. "We've no way to warn people without causing a panic. There are no precautions for them to take, no way of knowing how this illness is transmitted, or what treatments will be useful against it. Hell, if there's any point in treating them at all as far as that goes. There's a chance taking them to the hospital will be a waste of time."

Cecil said, "We have to tell them something. You make it sound as if we're looking at an outbreak. Word about that will spread fast no matter what we do, so we might as well take charge of it now. People are much more understanding of magic than they once were. If we tell them the illness is supernatural in origin, that may be enough to stem a panic."

Cora said, "As much as I hate to agree with Cecil, I think he's right."

Dorothy reluctantly nodded. "Go to the Inkwell and bring in as much of the Society as possible. Thank heavens we have all those former Elephants at our disposal. Even with their help, we may be stretched thin."

"Not to state the obvious," Cora said, "but is it really wise for us to gather in one place?"

Cecil realized what she was implying. "Oh, God." He rapidly pulled a handkerchief from his pocket and pressed it against the lower half of his face, backing away from the women with a terrified expression.

Dorothy rolled her eyes. "I was standing between Trafalgar and Violet when the curse exploded. If the illness has reached outside these walls, you're doomed already anyway. I'm not feeling any ill effects, Leonard seemed fine when he left..." She realized she didn't know for a fact Leonard was still healthy. "We should probably call to ensure he arrived safely at Wessex Base."

"Why would it skip over you?" Cecil asked.

"You ask me as if I know anything more about this than you do. I'm as lost in the dark as..." Her voice trailed off. "Wessex Base. Leonard and I were both there. If this curse is aware enough to know when Trafalgar arrived in London, then it stands to reason the curse must also know who was with her in Suffolk. Trafalgar and Violet fell because they were the ones who actually trespassed into the tomb. The rest of us, however... it wants us up and moving around. Spreading it to the rest of our army. We're disease vectors."

Cecil turned and ran from the room, muttering curses into his handkerchief.

Though irritated with him, Dorothy looked at Cora. "You should probably follow his lead."

Cora shook her head. "You were correct when you said anyone here is already infected with whatever we're up against. So the odds are that I get ill, like the women across the hall, or perhaps I've been chosen as one of these vectors to spread the infestation. Whichever it is, the safest place for me is at your side. So here I shall stay."

"Thank you, Cora. I wish I could reward your loyalty with some sort of rousing speech, but I don't think I have one in me."

"That's okay. You created the Mnemosyne Society to stand tall when you weren't able. It's about time we pulled our weight." She stood and stepped closer to the desk, putting her hand on top of Dorothy's. "Let me take the lead. I'll create a line of communication between here and the Keepings in Suffolk, and we can use the new recruits to monitor the outbreak. There are dozens of books at the Inkwell, and one of them is bound to have some useful information. We'll find it, you can be sure. We'll take care of everyone else's world." She gestured at the door. "You focus on taking care of yours."

Dorothy brought Cora's hand to her lips and kissed the back of it. "As you wish, fearless leader."

Cora lightly swatted Dorothy's cheek. "Sod off, you little bugger. You've carried us long enough. It's time for you to be selfish, and for the Society to do what you always intended. Protect the present from the threats of the past."

"If I must step back from a leadership role, then I suppose I can't think of anyone more capable of taking my place."

"Just don't step too far back. Judging from what we've already seen, we're going to need all the help we can muster to prevent this from becoming a catastrophe."

Dorothy pressed her lips together and nodded gravely. "And two of our best soldiers are out of commission. This is going to be a hell of a fight."

Cora nodded. "Then let's begin fighting."

Dorothy smiled and pushed herself up out of the chair.

"Let's."

## Chapter Eight

The unofficial number of afflicted Londoners rose to the double digits by evening. The next morning, it ballooned to the hundreds. Threadneedle was also not the only source of sufferers; they came from Spitalfields, Cripplegate, and even as far away as Clerkenwell. Dorothy had no doubt that before long they would hear reports from every district and estate in London. She also knew those numbers were misleading; they only represented people capable of getting themselves to the hospital and actually made the effort. There was no telling how many woke up ill and simply decided to stay in bed to see if it passed.

Was this disease clever enough to stop at the far reaches of London? How would someone cursing a tomb in the seventh century program their illness to follow the borders of a city so many centuries later? Was it somehow using Trafalgar's knowledge to spread itself? And if so, could they use that to make it stop? It was an idea worth exploring, though she couldn't see any practical application other than making Trafalgar believe London was destroyed.

She processed all of these thoughts at Trafalgar's bedside, holding her friend's limp hand, watching her face for any signs of waking. Other than a deepening layer of sweat and the occasional groan of pain, nothing changed. Violet was in equally bad shape, though she seemed to moan more frequently than Trafalgar. Was she in more pain? Or was Trafalgar better at hiding her discomfort even while unconscious? It was just one more unknown in a maddening series of them.

Cora and the rest of the Society were encamped at the Inkwell searching for any reference to a curse like this throughout history. Leonard and Agnes elected to remain in Suffolk and explore the site for anything that might help, and they reluctantly gave Cecil permission to access their home library to pore over the notes they'd left behind about Seaxburh.

While she sat with her friends, Dorothy mentally reviewed the Elephants. They had over thirty new recruits, all of them with some kind of supernatural ability, and one of them had to be of use in this situation.

They had put the women who were most reluctant to join up with Cecil. Trafalgar argued that it was more likely he would be corrupted by their influence rather than the egotistical fop guiding them onto the straight and narrow, but Dorothy thought it was the best fit. Leonard and Agnes would have acted like wardens, the women would have bristled, and no progress would be made in either direction. Cora would have been helpless to understand why anyone would choose a life of crime over being an upright member of society. But Cecil was generally a good man who had a flexible respect for law and order. The former criminals would see him as a kindred spirit.

Who was in his circle? She tried to remember names, abilities, any specifics. A woman named Madge White who could produce and control bursts of flame. Paula Hazlitt could see in the dark. Charlotte Fleming had the ability to look and sound like anybody, an ability that was alarming and astounding in equal measure, but nonetheless completely useless in their current situation. Cecil's group was good at brute force, sneakiness, destruction. They wouldn't know the first thing about healing.

Cora had someone who could heal. But only her own injuries, or illnesses she contracted. So she would likely be untouched by this curse. Eileen Fisk... couldn't she create some sort of energy projection field? Perhaps that would be useful in quarantining those who were already sick. It did nothing to solve the problem, of course, but it would at least prevent things from getting even worse.

She got to her feet and made a quiet noise of frustration. "We're surrounded by some of the most powerful and fantastic women who have ever existed, and every bloody one of them is absolutely useless in this crisis. Walk through walls, impenetrable skin, stretch your arm out the length of a damn city block. Wonderful in a sideshow attraction, but not exactly helpful to a real problem."

She went to the window and rested her hands on the sill. She could only see the brick wall and shaded windows of the building across the street, but she knew the city was continuing unchanged beyond it. Soon people would learn about the curse. More would fall ill, maybe some would die. When would it end? When it killed King George? Would it only be satisfied if it killed every British person in London?

"The Age of Magic," she muttered to her reflection, thinking of Riya Lennox's dire warning. "Lot of good it's doing us now."

The world would become dependent on magic, Riya had told them. Everyone using magic for the simplest of tasks. And then one day, she had refused to say how far in the future it was, magic would suddenly go away. It would be used up or abused to the point where it simply faded and left humanity helpless apes. She and Trafalgar had seen firsthand what could happen if someone overused magic. Beatrice was lying upstairs in a vegetative state because she didn't know when to stop.

Magic. She leaned forward and rested her head against the glass. Magic would make it so easy. Just wave her hands, say a spell, and the city would be healed. She pressed her lips together and shook her head. How many people were falling sick right now? How many Londoners were collapsing in pain, passing out in their homes and offices, with no idea what was happening to them? If there was a magical cure, wouldn't it be irresponsible to look the other way because of what might happen in the future?

She turned on the ball of her foot with the intention of going back into the library but was stopped short by the woman standing behind her. She wore a tight-fitting leather jacket and a floor-length dress which accentuated the curve of her hips. Her brown skin shone with sweat, and a few strands of black hair had fallen free around her face.

"Riya Lennox," Dorothy said. "I was wondering if you would show your face again."

"It's more difficult now. Divergent paths. We're not exactly on the same line anymore, but that can change in an instant."

Dorothy stepped closer. "Dancing back and forth through time, crossing alternate possibilities, 'fixing' your own timeline. That's your ability, isn't it?"

"I don't know what you mean."

"When we met, the Mnemosyne Society was just a handful of people chosen personally by Trafalgar and myself. We were only explorers, fascinated by the past and the hidden world of magic and monsters that came before ours. But now we're a much larger group. The vast majority of our members have some ability or another. Helena Swan can create blinding light from her palms. Eveline Barrington can shoot an acorn off a tree from across the river. And then there's Janya, with such uncanny agility she can scale walls and leap across rooftops like a cat. That would be Janya... Lennox, wouldn't it?"

Riya twisted her lips. The expression wasn't a smile or a grimace, but somewhere in between. Dorothy wasn't looking for a confirmation but that expression would have been all she needed.

"Janya is one of Cecil's wards, isn't she? God, I should have known putting him in charge of a dozen women would have been too much for his self-control."

"It wasn't sordid," Riya said. "Their relationship was consensual and resulted in a child. A child born with the ability to do wonderful, magical things. By the time she becomes pregnant, two-thirds of children will be born with some kind of magical ability. Her child could travel backward and forward through time using her bloodline."

"You said that fissures in reality were what allowed you to travel in time."

Riya shrugged. "That wasn't a lie. Those fissures, the tears created when the Great War normalized magical use, meant there were more children like me born every year. People who could see through walls or grew wings out of their backs. It's part of what led to the problems I warned you about. It's one thing to start using magic as an adult and then lose the ability. Can you imagine what it would be like to be born with magic and then have it taken away? It would be like going blind or deaf."

"So why have you returned now?"

"To stop you from making a horrible mistake. The problems began with the widespread use of magic in the Great War. Generals using it to win battle after battle, soldiers using it to mend broken bones, clear away storms, calm a sea. That was enough to forever change the world. It awoke the woman you called Virago and made her more powerful than she would have been otherwise. It created my grandmother and the other Elephants. It woke beasts which had been slumbering for millennia beneath the surface of the world."

"The Minotaur," Dorothy said, brushing past her to go into Trafalgar's room. "D'janira and her serpents."

Riya followed her. "And others you have yet to discover. The War weakened the barrier between their world and ours, but what you're considering will shatter it completely. Cracks can be healed, repaired, mended. What you want to do will change everything."

Dorothy wheeled around to face her. "Will it bring Trafalgar back? Will it help Beatrice wake up?"

"I'm asking you to consider the long-term.."

"Did this happen in your timeline? Seaxburh, the curse, Beatrice's coma. Did all of this happen?"

"Yes," Riya said, and then quickly added, "I hope you don't expect me to tell you—"

Dorothy closed the distance between them. "You're asking me to keep a weapon holstered. I need to know what the consequences will be. How many die from this curse?"

Riya looked past Dorothy, then down at the floor.

"Millions."

Dorothy reeled. "And Trafalgar?"

"She recovers. But she's... different. The illness weakens her, and she... she becomes a scholar. The work she does is invaluable to the Society." She could see Dorothy wasn't satisfied with that and reluctantly continued. "She never goes on another expedition. Violet also becomes infirm due to the curse. She is not as strong as Trafalgar, so it strikes her harder. She frequently becomes ill. Trafalgar takes care of her until she dies of pneumonia in a few years."

"God." Dorothy put a hand against the wall to support herself.

"And what of *you*, Lady Boone?" Her tone had changed, and she now sounded angry and bitter. "Are you curious about those answers?"

Dorothy said, "Why would you volunteer that information?"

"Because I want you to know that whatever decision you're about to make, you will have to live with it for a very long time. You're alive in my time."

"What? That's impossible. If your mother hasn't even been born yet..."

"Magic affects everyone it touches, Dorothy. For good or ill, no one comes away unchanged. You attain some small measure of immortality. There's obviously no way of knowing exactly how long you'll live, but you're in perfect health and look barely unchanged in my time. Well... perhaps I should say you haven't aged much, because you have definitely changed."

It wasn't difficult for Dorothy to guess what she meant. To live until the next century, decade upon decade of loss and pain and tragedy... She would be unrecognizable to herself.

"If magic is a finite resource," she said slowly, "then perhaps the best way to prevent it from becoming commonplace is to use as much as possible now. Summon everything we can to cure millions of Londoners against an ancient curse. Magic will be exhausted before it has a chance to get a foothold. Two birds with one stone."

"You're putting the future at risk!"

Dorothy shouted, "There is no such thing as the future! I don't care who you are, what you can do, or what you claim. The only thing that matters is right now, and I see a path to saving two women I love, and I will not waste time thinking about what *might* happen. There is now. That is what matters."

"The world will remember you for what do you next, Lady Boone. I pray they can forgive you."

"If what you say is true, I'll have plenty of time to regain their trust."

Dorothy waited for a retort and, when none came, she looked over her shoulder to see Riya had vanished. She sniffed derisively and looked into Trafalgar's room again.

"Good riddance, Miss Lennox."

She watched Trafalgar for another minute, then went to see what she could find in the archives.

## CHAPTER NINE

"HOLD UP," Cecil said. "Now you're saying we *can* use magic? You said we had to minimize our use by any means necessary!"

"The boy has a point," Agnes said. "After what happened to poor Beatrice, you and Trafalgar were very clear about your feelings toward Riya Lennox's plan to end magic."

"Circumstances have changed," Dorothy said.

The main room of the Inkwell was packed full of Mnemosyne Society members. Normally, Dorothy would have been invigorated to stand in a room with dozens of women and only two men present, but the circumstances were far too dire for any joy. She hated leaving Trafalgar, Beatrice, and Violet at the house, but other than dragging their unconscious bodies across town, she didn't have many options. One of the Florences had come back to London with the Keepings and offered to watch over them during the meeting.

Leonard and Agnes had returned from Suffolk for this meeting, and both looked weary to the bone. The stress they must have been under had to be immense. Dorothy couldn't imagine being in their situation. The curse had been unleashed because of their mission, their holy grail. They were the only two people present who would blame them for that, but Dorothy knew from experience that it was enough.

"We are facing a catastrophe, ladies. The death toll will be more than we can fathom. And those who survive will be forever changed in the aftermath. We can stop that. There is still time to stop it, to put things right. Who has been monitoring the hospitals?"

Alice Nobbs, one of Cora's apprentices, lifted her hand. She was a very slight creature, bony limbed with big eyes and a hangdog expression.

"I've been covering as much as I can. I have, um, I can see imminent deaths? A dark aura. There are some at St. Luke's. But no, I d-don't think anyone has died so far."

"But soon," Dorothy said.

Alice nodded. "Yes'm. People are going to start dyin' soon."

Polly Kitchen, a woman who could convince people to do almost anything she asked, said, "I got the doctors to tell me that they've got patients from all over London now. It's only been one day, but every borough is accounted for. They're already running low on medicine, not to say anything about beds. They don't have a clue what they're going to do if the numbers keep climbing."

"And the numbers will keep climbing," Dorothy said. "That is the one thing we can guarantee if we keep spinning our wheels. Leonard, Agnes, have you made any progress at the site?"

Leonard said, "We've found inscriptions along the inside of the hull. We're working to translate them, but we're confident that it's how the curse was set."

"If you finish the translation, do you believe there will be a way to reverse the effects?" Dorothy asked.

"Yes," Leonard said, then glanced at Agnes. "But even with Sadie and the Florences, it will take time. Time that I don't believe we can spare."

"I concur," Dorothy said. "Which brings us to why I've asked you all to be here this evening. The Society has greatly benefited by taking money from Riya Lennox to end magic. If we do this, she could very well end those payments. Hell, we're talking about a time-traveler here. She may find a way to make it so that we never had the money in the first place. I don't know what's going to happen. But using magic on such a large scale could have unintended personal consequences. I want to be certain we're all agreed, because it will affect all of us."

One of Cecil's apprentices, Charlotte Fleming, said, "We all get an equal vote?"

Dorothy remembered Charlotte. They had butted heads when she was still loyal to Maud Keaton. "The past is a different country, Miss Fleming," Dorothy said. "You are now a member of this Society and you will be given a voice equal to the rest of us." She looked at the faces around the room. "Unless anyone else has further questions, I say we bring it to a vote. All those in favor of using magic to end this blasted curse, think affirmatively."

She looked at Angel Tuffin, the gentle giant who had saved Trafalgar's life when she was captured by the other Elephants. Angel scanned the crowd, then nodded to Dorothy.

"All those against..."

"Mum?" Angel said, almost sheepishly. "We already have a very large majority. Only a couple didn't vote affirmative-like."

"Oh, I see. Thank you, Angel. Those who abstained or planned to say no, would you like a chance to argue your case?"

No one moved, no one spoke, and Angel shook her head to indicate no one was sending her particularly loud messages.

"Then I say this matter is settled. Let's fight magic with magic."

Cecil cleared his throat and leaned forward. "Obviously I support the general idea. Hurrah, going rogue and breaking the rules. It's all well and good to say we fight magic with magic, but how exactly? We've been fighting pretty hard so far and we ain't made so much as a dent, love."

Cora said, "He's not wrong, Dorothy. We have a lot of talent here and I'm still not sure we have much of a chance to stop this."

"We're talking about magic here, Miss Hyde," an apprentice named Alma Jessup said. "I can walk through walls. Myra can breathe underwater as well as any fish." She nodded across the room. "And Izzie has that unbreakable skin. There's got to be something we can do."

A woman from Cecil's group sighed. "Cease, I know you told me to keep quiet, but I have to tell 'em. I can heal people."

Dorothy frowned. "What? You're, ah, Edith Bowles. You told us that your ability was... ah..."

"Golems, ma'am," Edith said. "But since we've been working with Cease, I've found another ability."

Cecil said, "Edith, you don't have to do this."

"Yeah, I do." She sighed and pressed her lips together. "I can heal people."

"A bruised arm," Cecil said, glaring at Edith. "Headaches, cramping, that sort of thing. And even doing that leaves you lightheaded. This is a whole level of magnitude different, love."

Dorothy said, "I'm afraid he's correct. Healing one person's minor ailment is nothing compared to an epidemic. It's as if saying you can carry ten books at once, so you're going to try lifting the entire library."

Edith stepped forward. "I'd like to try. I can pull back~"

"I said *no!*"

Dorothy snapped the last word so loudly that half the women in the room leaned away from her. Edith's eyes widened and she retreated a step, but Dorothy held up a hand in apology.

"Please forgive me. I'm... I'm..."

"A very dear friend of ours overextended herself recently," Cora explained gently. "Dorothy has seen the damage it can cause firsthand. I don't think any of us are willing to risk having it happen again."

Dorothy nodded to her. "Thank you, Cora. We won't get anywhere with brute force. Whatever happened to Trafalgar and Violet in that tomb was the catalyst for all of this. A person can't be healthy one moment and then deathly ill the next without some sort of supernatural intervention. Seaxburh or those loyal to her laid a magical trap."

Agnes said, "We'll go back to the site and finish our work to find out exactly how this trap was laid, and once we know that, we'll know how to fight it."

"We can only hope," Dorothy said. "In the meantime, everyone here... continue doing whatever you can. Even if you think your abilities are worthless at a time like this, you must try. Strength can be used to set up a triage unit. Controlling the weather can lower the temperature of a room where a dozen people are running a fever. Who can project invisible energy barriers?" A woman raised her hand. "You can put mobile quarantines around doctors tending to patients."

Cora stood. "We'll figure it out. Right now we're on a time table and we have no idea how long we have before people start dying from this illness. Get yourself to Suffolk, Lady Boone. We'll hold down the fort here."

"Thank you, Cora."

She scanned the other faces in the room. Most of them were still strangers to her, though she'd tried her best to at least learn their names. Mabel, Alice, Honour, Eileen, the twins Phoebe and Pamela, Eveline, Selina, Susannah... They were scarred, some of them bore marks of broken noses or misshapen eye sockets. Lives lived roughly, she had very recently been their enemy. Now she was entrusting the safety of London to them.

"Thank you," she said. "All of you. Your work here, your sacrifices, will not be forgotten. This fight is yours, and so should the rewards. You are no longer apprentices of the Mnemosyne Society. You are all full members in good standing."

Agnes smiled proudly at her group, then gestured at the door. "Shall we, Lady Boone?"

Dorothy nodded and put on her riding cap. "Let's get to work."

Not terribly far from where the recently inflated Mnemosyne Society met in the Inkwell, the woman known as the Dov was sequestered in her library searching for something she prayed she wouldn't find. Years ago, Bao Tai Sek - also called Beatrice Sek, colloquially known as 'Trix' by those she loved - had come to her and asked about a prophecy. The Dov told her what she knew, revealed to Beatrice that she was one of four elementals. She represented earth, and drew power from that source. Dirt, stone, roots. The others were fire, water, and wind. Their awakening was meant to signal the beginning of a great magical age.

The Great War brought magic back into the world. Since then, three of the elementals had been identified. Lasair, the fire elemental, was dead at the hand of the water elemental, Emmeline Potter, who in turn was dead at the hand of Beatrice Sek. They had yet to identify the wind elemental, but the Dov knew she was out there. Somewhere.

According to the prophecy, when the four elementals were reunited, they would bring about a fifth element: void. But what would happen if all four of the harbingers of the great magical age died? She knew Lady Boone was attempting to destroy magic entirely, but she could feel power swelling in the ether. London's energy was swelling like a tide behind a dam, and she was terrified that Boone and her novices would inadvertently doom the entire world with their flailing.

The Dov could find nothing to tell her what to expect if Beatrice died. She could find no book or tablet or prophecy that laid out a world where magic was forced back into its bottle. She feared it would be like trying to stifle a grenade by throwing it into a campfire.

Too much was at risk for her to sit and hope everything worked out for the best. She closed her eyes and summoned enough energy to take her back to Threadneedle, arriving in the upper-floor hallway outside of Bao Tai Sek's sickroom. She paused and listened until she pinpointed the only other conscious person in the house. Not really a person at all, but a magical construct. That made it easy. She felt around the edges of the golem and pulled. The artificial girl gasped once, and then dissipated into the energy that had been used to create her.

Once that was done, the Dov held out her hand with the palm upturned. She curled her fingers and took a deep breath as she felt around the edges of the house's energy.

"I know you are here, Bao Tai Sek. I know that if I force you back into your body before it has healed, I will only damage you. But I must bind you to your mortal frame. It will not be comfortable but it must be done. Otherwise you will be left behind, and that would have dire consequences."

She felt a presence beside her. She could almost hear the words being spoken, though they were said on another plane.

"I am protecting you. That is all. You came to me for help years ago. I am finally prepared to grant your request, at a time when it is needed the most."

The Dov lowered her hand. The spirit followed her into the bedroom. The Dov sensed screaming, resistance, but she ignored it. She took a deep breath and swept her hands up. The dirt that appeared came from the garden below, causing an immediate sinkhole to appear as it formed a shell around the body lying in the bed. More dirt appeared and the muddy chrysalis grew larger. The Dov pressed the air in front of her and the dirt compacted tighter, squeezing Beatrice's body to the point of harm.

When she was finished, the dirt shell sat on top of the mattress like an immense cigar. It was packed tightly enough that tools would have been required to begin breaking through. The Dov looked at it with a touch of regret.

"This is for the best," she whispered, hoping somehow Lady Boone would understand that when she returned and found the bed empty.

With a quick gesture of one hand, the Dov vanished.

The dirt-encased body of Beatrice Sek went with her.

## Chapter Ten

THERE WAS mud in the bed.

The Florence they'd left watching the house was gone, even though the other Florence insisted she should have lasted a few more hours, and there was mud in the bed.

Dorothy stared at it with no expression on her face, but inside she raged. She'd confirmed Trafalgar and Violet were still there, and now she tried to push away her emotions and approach the situation with calm rationality. She worked her jaw, stared without blinking, flexed and relaxed her hands, struggling to keep her breathing steady. The air of the house buzzed with the remnants of powerful magic, just as it had after the Dov's previous visit.

She heard Cora's footsteps in the hall. She paused in the doorway, then came closer to stand at Dorothy's shoulder. They stared at the bed together.

"No one on the street saw anything," she said as if afraid of waking a sleeper. "Of course they all have concerns of their own, since this was where the epidemic began."

Dorothy said, "It was the witch. Renata Koessel. She told me burying Trix was the only way to heal her. I was... I planned to find a way to do it, but then Agnes called about Trafalgar and I rushed to help her, and I just haven't had the time to..." She ran out of breath and closed her eyes, sagging forward. Cora stepped closer and put an arm around her. "I'm going to lose everyone. Aren't I? Everyone who matters to me will be gone."

"May I be cruel?" Cora asked. "Just for a moment?"

"You? Cruel?"

Cora took Dorothy's hand. "You are not the only one who has

suffered. Sacrificed. Lost. Suffered." Dorothy tried to pull her hand away, but Cora held tight. "I'm not trying to diminish what you've gone through. What you're going through. I watched as three women who trusted me disappeared into a cavern and were never seen again. Leonard and Agnes have lost more than I can begin to list. We've all been shattered. We've all lost people dear to us. But we're stronger at the broken places. I'm not telling you to stop being sad. I still mourn for the girls I left behind. I'm only saying... don't stop fighting. Don't blind yourself with what you've lost so you can't see what needs to be done."

This time Cora didn't fight when Dorothy let go of her hand. They stood in awkward silence before Cora sighed softly.

"I'll gather your things, in case you have to stay in Suffolk..."

She was at the door when Dorothy said, "Trafalgar saw her friend shot in the head."

Cora turned. "Pardon?"

"A bullet met for Trafalgar killed her friend. It happened right before we started working together. It was actually the *reason* we began working together. Trafalgar mourned, yes, but she did what was necessary. I have no doubt she would be doing the same thing now if our positions were reversed." She wiped away her tears and turned to face Cora. "Thank you for your cruelty. If it should become necessary again, I pray you don't wait until you're given permission to slap some sense into me."

Cora half-smiled and nodded. "It's not exactly in my nature, but I'll do my best."

Dorothy looked at the bed one more time. The Dov was almost a complete unknown, but she was the closest thing they had to an expert in Beatrice's condition. Whatever was happening, whatever had been done, she could only have faith that the woman she loved was in good hands. Finally she turned away. She would waste no more time on sorrow when there was still a chance to save everyone. She hold back on her pain until the job was done.

She looked at her hands again. The skin prickled with leftover magic. Being in the presence of magic, even if the user had been gone for hours, was like feeling a rainstorm building in the atmosphere. She tilted her head to the side as she considered that, flexed her fingers and watched them move. The air was different... physically different, and even a non-user could detect that oddness. An idea sparked, and she moved quicker to catch up with Cora.

"Let's go, Miss Hyde," she said. "We have a long train ride ahead of us and I believe I've inadvertently discovered a clue that might help us. We may not even have to use magic at all to put everything right."

Cora followed her into the hall. "That's fantastic. How in the world do you intend to do that?"

"I plan to ask a ghost very nicely to take back her curse."

Cora blinked, skeptical, but continued following Dorothy down the stairs.

The interior of the ship was musty with the scent of wet earth and plant rot. Dorothy descended into the pit via rope, scanning the space illuminated by the torch on her belt. When she reached the bottom, she unfastened the harness and looked up to see Cora and two Florences peering down at her. She gave them a thumbs-up and took a moment to look around the space for signs of the flood Trafalgar and Violet had mentioned. The curved wooden ribs of the ship were almost completely reclaimed by roots and soil, but they appeared to be intact. She could also see carved shapes on each plank, but the wood was so ancient that she couldn't begin to decipher it.

"Few magic spells survive their incantation being destroyed," she said, mostly to herself but loudly enough that the women on the surface could hear. "Whatever Trafalgar and Violet triggered, I don't think it was summoned by what's written on the walls."

"There's also writing on the tomb itself," Florence called down. "Trafalgar said that's where they was standing when Violet first saw the illusion."

"If illusion is indeed what it was," Dorothy muttered.

She walked to one side of the hull, giving the tomb a wide berth, and placed her hand on the wood. She could feel how weak it was, knew she could make it crumble with the slightest pressure. It was fascinating how the ground had reclaimed the ship. It almost looked like a natural formation, some quirk of ecology that happened to create a void within a hill in the shape of a boat.

It had been waiting here for thirteen hundred years, give or take. The magic would have to be colossal to still be active in the modern day, to still have enough power to cause an epidemic. For that much magical energy to be buried in a hole, just waiting... there must be something lingering in the space. The ship had become part of the earth, and it stood to reason the magic would have seeped into its bones as well. But she couldn't feel anything. No frisson of energy, no sense of power. All she felt was mold and decay.

Dorothy turned and walked to the tomb. She stood at the foot and placed her palms flat on its lid. She pushed, the muscles of her shoulders strained, but she didn't let up.

The woman appeared directly opposite from her, at the tomb's head. She looked the same as she had in the foyer at Threadneedle, but she seemed to be looking directly at Dorothy.

"We are kin," she said, "so I shall give you one chance to leave this place."

"The hell you will," Dorothy said. "I've come to speak with you, 'your highness', and I'm not leaving without some answers."

"Depart this place with no more than you brought. Tell no one what you've found."

Dorothy stepped around the tomb. "We can drop the charade, love. The kind of magic required for a curse like this would leave a footprint. This whole area would be awash with the energy spilling out of the grave. Trees, flowers, even the damn grass would be imbued with the essence of the magic waiting here to catch potential grave robbers. But everything up there is ordinary. Trafalgar never mentioned it, and she would have made a note of how it felt. This room should feel like part of another world. Instead it feels like just another hole in the ground."

The woman may have flinched. Dorothy pressed on.

"It's peculiar... unless the magic was dormant. Unless there was no spell waiting to be unleashed. Unless it was a creature lying in wait to attack."

Seaxburh continued to stare straight ahead, despite the fact Dorothy was at her elbow.

"Red hair, dressed in white, short stature. We're a long way from Ireland, but I think I'm looking at a banshee."

The woman turned to look at her, all artifice gone from her face and posture. There was no doubt now that she could see Dorothy.

"Your country is already facing the consequences for trespassing on these sacred grounds. I don't see any benefit from twice cursing you."

"I didn't come here to tempt fate or to steal the treasure. I came to convince you to reverse the damage you've already done."

The banshee faced forward again and began fading from sight. Dorothy reached into her pouch, withdrew a small metallic canister. She held it out away from her body.

"I assume you haven't seen one of these before, so let me explain what I'm about to do. This is a Wonderlite. All I have to do is flick my thumb on the little wheel like this, and scratches an alloy, which creates a spark. And well..."

She flicked the lighter and a flame leapt up. The banshee solidified and stared at the fire, then looked at Dorothy with rage in her eyes.

"You dare..."

"You're damned right I dare. You threaten the people I care about, I have no qualms about burning the remains of the queen you've spent a thousand years guarding."

"I will grant you immortality and curse you with every plague known to mankind."

Dorothy's blood chilled at the threat, remembering Riya Lennox's assertion that she did indeed gain immortality at some point. But she maintained eye contact. Her arm didn't waver above the tomb.

"We did not come here to thieve, or to damage your queen's final resting place. Two people dedicated their entire lives to finding Seaxburh and finally cementing her place in history. Anything they would have taken from this tomb would have been used to confirm her legacy."

"So you claim."

"We're explorers," Dorothy said. "We try to ensure the things we uncover are returned to their rightful owners. These treasures..." She turned and shone her flashlight over the items. "The things left here are relics of an era lost to history. We could learn so much about where we came from, the people we came from. You wish to protect her...? You're ensuring that she will remain forgotten, brushed aside by the men who wrote about that era. Somehow I don't believe that is what you actually want."

The banshee looked at the tomb. Finally, she spoke in a low whisper.

"Seaxburh was kind to me. She was kind to all the Sidhe, We were hated and feared by kings and the men who followed them, but she knew how to respect the unknown without fighting or exploiting it. When she assumed power, she promised to protect us. She was meant to have a long, powerful reign." She worked her jaw. Tears filled her eyes. "Men would not allow that to come to pass. She ruled for a little over a year before they finally displaced her. She was forced to battle every day just to keep power. Eventually she failed and they removed her from the throne. Their campaign to erase her legacy began immediately. One day a queen, the following she was no more than a beggar."

"You're the ones who buried her here. The... the Sh-ith-ee."

She wasn't certain she'd gotten the pronunciation right, but the banshee nodded.

"We offered retribution against her enemies. Plagues. Death. Pain. Seaxburh was compassionate, even in defeat. She denied our request. She grew old. She watched her name erased from memory. And then one day, she died. And only her friends in the Sidhe mourned her."

"I'm sorry," Dorothy said.

"We made a vow to stand watch over her. Waiting for the day an enemy would attempt to desecrate her remains. We knew they would come. We vowed we would be ready for them."

Dorothy felt her hopes rising. "I'm sorry to say that there are still people who might not like the idea of a queen. But we can make them sit down and listen if we have the evidence to back up the story. We can use all of this to ensure Seaxburh is given her proper respect."

The banshee looked up, as if she could see through the wood and soil. For all Dorothy knew, she could.

"You swear on your soul that these people are trustworthy?"

"The people who have spent their entire lives searching for Seaxburh, yes. They would do anything to protect her legacy. Yes. I would weigh my life against their honor."

"Very well. I will shall grant passage to them and their envoys." The banshee sounded incredibly weary, and her face seemed to have aged decades in the past few moments. She leaned heavily on her sword, staring at the tomb. Finally, she gave a small smile. "You will be known, my queen. At long last, you will stand in the light."

Dorothy let her enjoy the moment before she cleared her throat. "There's just the small matter of the curse..."

"I will not place the curse on anyone who enters this tomb."

"Yes, that's understood. But... the illness continues to spread in London." The banshee furrowed her brow and looked at Dorothy, clearly not understanding her. "The women who came here before. The ones you infected..."

"Yes...?"

Dorothy said, "We've come to an agreement. The Keepings are working in Seaxburh's best interest. The curse was wrongly placed. You must lift it before people begin dying for no reason."

The banshee shook her head. "I apologize, Lady Boone. We do have an agreement, but the trap was set and triggered. It's a boulder rolling downhill. Once it has been set in motion, it cannot be stopped. I am sorry about your cohorts, but there is nothing to be done. The sickness cannot be reversed."

## CHAPTER ELEVEN

THE FIRST death was reported while Dorothy was traveling back to London. An elderly man from Whitechapel was already in poor health when he was stricken by what the press was already calling 'the Modern Plague.' She knew it was only a matter of time before able-bodied victims began succumbing as well. Trafalgar was healthy, and Violet seemed sturdy enough, but she couldn't waste any time.

She had a plan. Or rather the shape of a plan, a terrible idea that had the benefit of being their only option. She spent the train ride home scouring the list of new Mnemosyne Society members and their powers to see if any could be utilized for what she was thinking.

Cecil's apprentice Edith Bowles could heal minor injuries. Dorothy would ask her to focus that ability on Florence Barbour, who was the key to the whole plan. One person could only channel so much magic. But if that person was actually a dozen people or two dozen, each one could be filled to the limit. And since the duplicates were pure magical energy, it would boost the power. She felt guilty about essentially murdering a large group of women, but Florence assured her that shouldn't be an issue.

"Honestly, they die in all kinds of silly ways. At least this has the benefit of being unique and serving a purpose."

They would be paired with Mabel Howes, another apprentice of the Keepings. Her ability was to enhance the powers of others around her. Agnes didn't know the exact mathematics of it, but she guessed any ability was increased by a power of ten when Mabel was in the same room. So she would have Mabel increasing Edith's healing power to channel it through a dozen Florences, each channeling the maximum amount of magical energy a human could hold, and Mabel would increase that by ten for each one.

The last piece of the puzzle was one of Cora's ladies, a brutish brawler called Honour Battle. She could control the weather. Once the women were using their powers, she would use the wind to spread it across London with a focus on the most affected areas.

Dorothy tapped her pen against her teeth. It would have to be enough. It was a massive, massive use of magical energy. It was precisely what Riya Lennox had warned them about, and what she and Trafalgar had sworn to combat. But could she really allow London to fall in order to protect the future? Millions of people would die. One of the largest cities in the world, wiped off the map in the blink of an eye. Surely that would damage Riya's precious future as much or more than magic.

Besides, now they were forewarned. They knew the threat existed. They could campaign for a reasonable use of magic from here on out. Regulation, moderation. Science and technology would continue to progress just as it always had, but now there would be a gentle boost. London would live. Humanity would thrive. All she had to do was create a tidal wave of magic to heal a city. By the time she stepped off the train, she was determined that everything would be back to normal very soon.

This would not be their final adventure together. She would make certain of that.


"Is it dangerous?"

"Well, that's a stupid question," Cecil said.

Cora glared at him. They were back in the Inkwell, but now it was just the founding members of the Society, minus the obvious absences of Abraham, Trafalgar, and Beatrice.

"Of course it's dangerous at the core of it. What I'm asking is how dangerous is it? The girls have a right to know what sort of risk we're asking them to take."

"Seems like we have two options," Cecil said. "Either we try this, and yeah, one or two of 'em might get hurt. Sounds like all of the Florences except the original are being used like cannon fodder. Gonna burn 'em out like kindling. Maybe one of the others will get a headache or pass out. But the alternative is we just sit around and wait to get sick like everyone else. Then we all die anyway, without even trying to do anything. Doesn't seem like much of a choice to me."

Cora crossed her arms. "You do have a valid point, I suppose."

Dorothy finally spoke up. "We must leave it up to them. As you said, Cora, it's dangerous on the face of it. We cannot make this decision for them. If we did that, we might as well order them to do it, and then we'd be no better than Maud Keaton."

Leonard, who had been watching the back-and-forth from a booth with

Agnes, said, "What if just one of them refuses? I know you already spoke to Florence and she agreed, but the others are equally vital to the success of the plan. It's impossible without them."

"Then we will find another way," Dorothy said. "We will *not* force this on anyone."

Cecil cleared his throat. "One last thing, love. Four of our apprentices pushing themselves to the extent of their powers, plus however many Florences we end up using. And the end result will be hundreds if not thousands of people being healed by magic. That's a pretty big output."

"You're wrong on one count, Mr. Dubourne," Dorothy said. "It won't be hundreds or thousands. It will be millions. This cure must reach everyone in London, because that is who the curse targeted. Everyone is a potential victim, whether they're showing symptoms or not, and those who don't get sick are likely to be carriers of the disease. They all must be targeted. It will be the single largest magical event since the end of the war. Perhaps even larger than any of those campaigns." She paused and looked down at her shoes.

"Doing this will effectively kill our mission to end magic. But it will ensure London's survival."

Cecil blew out air past his lips, but couldn't quite make it a whistle. "Blimey. No pressure on us, then." He turned and paced toward the far wall, arms crossed. "Look, I didn't like it when you saddled me with a dozen little harpies. But they've grown on me. I care about them, and having Edith do something like this before she's ready... and I don't think she's ready, let me be clear about that. She makes golems, brings them to life. This healing thing is new. And if something went wrong, I'd... I..."

"My god," Cora gasped. "Dorothy, you've given Cecil empathy! The boy is finally growing up."

He made an obscene gesture at her.

Agnes said, "Cecil, your concerns are admirable. But you must ask yourself if you would rather watch Janya get sick, suffer, and die, along with all the other girls."

His eyes widened in surprise, narrowed in suspicion, and then he turned away. He worked his jaw. When he spoke again, his voice was rough. "Like you said. Ain't really up to me. We'll let Edith decide. But we're going to tell her all the risks. No kid gloves, no nothing."

"Absolutely."

"Then what are we doing wasting time here, then?" he said. "Let's call in the girls."

Dorothy said, "Yes, but not here. The curse started at the front step of my Threadneedle house, and that is where we should start the healing."

Cora nodded. "Makes sense to me."

"But you were right about one thing, Cecil." Dorothy squeezed his arm as she passed him. "We haven't a moment to waste."

The majority of the Society showed up to offer support to the four who would be taking part in the cure. They gathered in the street outside Dorothy's townhouse in a wide circle with the women of the hour standing in the center. They left enough room for Florence to create as many duplicates as she could without getting lightheaded. The previous record was twenty-eight, but she felt she could go a little higher under the circumstances. Dorothy told her not to push it and stick to twenty.

When everyone was ready, Dorothy nodded. Florence punched her palm, and immediately split off into a second person. They both hit their palms, and two more Florences appeared. Dorothy watched, fascinated despite her desperation. There was a slightly twinning of every feature on one Florence before the other appeared. It was a blur, almost imperceptible to the naked eye, but it was very obvious once she knew what to look for.

Soon, twenty Florences stood in the circle. Dorothy stepped back and waved Edith Bowles forward. She closed her eyes and held her hands out toward the main Florence.

Next came Mabel Howse, who stood between Florence and Edith and put a hand on both of their shoulders. She closed her eyes. Edith gasped and squared her shoulders, stood up straighter, and her entire body trembled. Florence gasped as well and her face almost seemed to glow. The other Florences also shone with this new light.

The air was electric. Dorothy felt the hair on her arms standing up in response. She knew everyone else was feeling the same thing, because she had to snap her fingers to get Honour Battle's attention. The big woman stepped into position, raised her hands to the sky like she was trying to catch a bird, and spread her fingers in a wide fan.

Everyone gathered felt the wind shift. It swirled a cyclone around them, whistled in their ears, and then lifted so suddenly that for a moment the world went silent. Dorothy looked up, half expecting to see a monsoon of magical energy above their heads, but the sky was clear. It was hard to catch her breath and she knew Honour had sucked most of the air from the street. But it was fine... it would be okay... She could already breathe easier as more air moved in to fill the vacuum.

"All across London," Dorothy said, her voice barely more than a gasp. "You must..."

"I've got it, mum," Honour muttered. She sounded like she was holding up a wall that had collapsed on her back. "Lemme concentrate..."

Dorothy pressed her lips together and looked at the other women. The Florences were turning to dust. She couldn't count how many they'd lost, but they were fading quickly.

The main Florence opened her eyes and met Dorothy's gaze. "More," she mouthed.

Dorothy frowned at her. "Are you..."

"*More.*"

Dorothy stepped forward and slapped Florence. Another appeared right beside her.

"Need more," Florence gasped. Her words were rushed, frantic, and sweat poured down her face. "Else all the energy's going through me. Can't handle that. I'll burn to a crisp. I need more, can't do it myself. Please, Lady Boone."

"I'm so sorry." Dorothy slapped Florence again, then again, and more duplicates appeared. For each one that was created, another fell. Dorothy's palm stung and her arm quickly became sore, but she couldn't stop. She had to keep up with the attrition rate. She switched hands, and soon both sides of Florence's face were pink, radiating heat. Dorothy felt tears on her cheeks as she slapped the poor girl again, and again, and again.

And then... silence and stillness. She stopped mid-strike and looked up, then looked at Edith. "What happened?" she asked.

"That's all we could... give." Edith collapsed, and Dorothy caught her before she could hit the ground. Honour swayed on her feet but was held up by a few of her friends. Mabel also looked absolutely drained, eyes blank and fingers twitching by her sides.

But Florence... Dorothy looked at her, cradling the girl's face with both hands. She was so young. Dorothy had known she was young, but she'd stopped seeing her as a child at some point. Now she saw the youth. The pain was too great for her to put on the airs of an adult. She gripped the collar of Dorothy's shirt, trembling in her arms as the last of her duplicates faded away to nothing.

"Did we do it?" Florence asked, her voice weak. "Did... did we win?"

Dorothy stroked the cheek she had bruised with her slapping. "We'll soon find out, love."

The air around her hummed with voices, a steady buzz of several speakers, all women. The voices blended together into nonsense songs punctuated by footsteps and doors closing. She was aware of a pressure in her head and intense heat. She dreamed she was in a cave with the door sealed by stone, hunched down, arms around her knees, waiting. The cave became smaller and smaller until she could feel the rough walls pressing down on her shoulders. The heat was more intense with each wave, but she couldn't move to wipe the stinging sweat out of her eyes.

And then, relief. It came on slowly at first, but the reversal was impossible to miss. She relaxed her shoulders. She was able to sit up straighter, and then the illusion faded. She knew she was lying in a bed, covered by a lightweight sheet. The euphony of sound became distinct voices, the voices of people she knew and loved.

The first time she opened her eyes, someone was standing in the doorway of the bedroom, a blur of yellow clothes and dark hair. She blinked and the person vanished, but someone was sitting beside the bed. A hand was holding hers, and she instinctively closed her fingers around it.

"Trafalgar?" Dorothy's voice was soft, hopeful. She put a hand on Trafalgar's forehead, and the palm felt gloriously cold against her overheated skin.

It took a tremendous effort to open her eyes and keep them open long enough to focus. She was rewarded by the sight of Dorothy Boone's worried face breaking into a relieved smile.

"Hello." Trafalgar's voice was rough, dry, and she pressed her lips together and swallowed hard. "Have I been ill?"

"Yes, love," Dorothy said, tears rolling down her cheeks now. "How do you feel now?"

Trafalgar carefully shook her head. "Unclear. But I think... improving." She realized there was someone beside her in the bed. She looked over and saw Violet. Her face was flushed, her hair darkened by sweat. "Violet...?"

"She's improving as well. They're all improving."

Trafalgar looked at Dorothy again. "All...? Who else was sick?"

Dorothy shook her head. "That can wait. For now, you're not entirely out of the woods. Rest. We can go over everything when you're better."

She stood and leaned over the bed to kiss Trafalgar's forehead.

"Everything is going to be fine now."

Trafalgar was still woozy, but she still couldn't mistake the lie hiding under Dorothy's words. "Something happened..."

"Nothing you need to concern yourself with now. It's over."

Another lie. But Trafalgar was already having difficulty keeping her eyes open. She knew she wouldn't go back to the cave, knew this would be a restful and restorative sleep, and she took Dorothy's hand in her own.

"Thank you," she whispered. "For whatever you did."

She was almost certain that the last thing she saw before closing her eyes was a look of guilt passing over Dorothy's face.

## CHAPTER TWELVE

WHEN THE dust settled, the citizens of London were more than willing to simply forget about their brush with calamity. There was no official death count from the mysterious outbreak, but Leonard deduced from public records that nearly two hundred and thirty people succumbed to the illness. The authorities attempted to find the source of the outbreak but, when they narrowed it down to Threadneedle Street, the investigation suddenly came to an end. Dorothy told Trafalgar that she assumed whoever was in charge decided she was also behind the disease being cured and decided to leave well enough alone.

It had rained every day since the cure. Thick black clouds appeared over the Thames, despite forecasts calling for clear skies, and the torrent hadn't let up since. Agnes believed it was a result of Honour manipulating the atmosphere in such a massive way and insisted it would pass in time.

Violet woke up the day after Trafalgar. She was gaunt and pale, but she smiled when she saw who was sharing the bed with her. They were alone in the room, since Cora had finally convinced Dorothy that everyone in the house needed to rest. Violet rolled onto her side with great care and gently touched her fingers to Trafalgar's lips.

"I dreamt I was in a great storm," she whispered in her weak voice. "Thunder crashing, lightning, and floodwaters rising. But I was safe under an outcropping of stone."

Trafalgar smiled. "Was I the stone?"

"I like to believe so."

"So would I. How do you feel?"

"Weak. But I can tell that I'm getting stronger. What happened?"

Trafalgar shook her head. "They haven't told me the details yet. I imagine it was something of great importance. Dorothy says we were only unconscious for a few days, but I feel we missed some grand developments. At the moment, I am content to lie here and not know for a while, until my constitution improves."

"I feel the same."

She stared at Trafalgar as if trying to memorize her features. They listened to the soft drumming of rain on the window, the occasional growl of thunder that echoed through the streets and rattled the windows. There were other people in the house - many of them, from the sound of it - but Trafalgar was only focused on the woman in front of her.

"Can I be frank?" Violet asked.

"With me, always."

Violet bit her lip and considered what she wanted to say before she spoke. "I don't have much in the way of religion. I never really thought about what happens next, where people go. But I felt like maybe that storm was happening in a place that isn't here. Purgatory, Hell, whatever you want to call it. Some place that's not here, some place that's after. I don't have regrets. I try to live my life so I don't need to wonder about what might have been. But I had a regret when I was there. I regretted never kissing you. I don't know if you sorted out your situation, and I respect if you haven't, and a kiss can just be a kiss, but I would really like to kiss you right now."

"I would like that very much. And just so there's no misunderstanding, my situation has been sorted out. It would be very okay if this was more than just a kiss."

She saw a flicker of relief and excitement pass over Violet's face before she leaned in. Their lips met only softly, it was as much as either of them could muster, but to Trafalgar it was as restorative as any medicine. She put her hand into the back of Violet's head and tangled her fingers in the curls. This was different than kissing Dorothy or Beatrice. There was passion in those kisses, oh was there passion, but with this kiss, she realized she only wanted to share that with one person. And she wanted to be the only person who received it from someone else.

The kiss broke and Violet sighed. She pressed her forehead against Trafalgar's. "I'm more than a fan of your work," she confessed. "I've been drawn to you since the moment I saw you. When I was a thief, just some guttersnipe not worth anyone's attention. I saw you leave a restaurant. In your fine coat. Standing tall. You had hair then, and it was in a long braid that swept to and fro when you walked. You were a goddess to me. I never thought I'd get a chance to speak to you, let alone..." She exhaled sharply in either a laugh or a sob, and shook her head. "Getting sick almost seems worth it to be here." She looked around and added, "Wherever here is."

Trafalgar said, "Oh... it's my bedroom."

Violet's eyes widened as she processed that. "Oh. So this would be your bed."

"That would be the logic, yes."

"I see. Well, well. Look at me now."

Trafalgar laughed. "Now that I've granted your wish, perhaps you could give me one."

"Anything."

"I would like to kiss *you*."

Violet blushed beneath her freckles. "I suppose that would only be fair."

They kissed again, and took their time with it.

Dorothy watched the rain washing down the parlor window, so lost in her thoughts that she didn't hear Cora enter the room and stand beside her. "There are reports," Cora said, ignoring the hitch in Dorothy's shoulders when she realized she was no longer alone, "that the first sizable magic campaigns during the Great War were accompanied by similar storms. Entire battlefields turned into swamps. Soldiers were sinking up to their knees in mud."

"When did the storms end?" Dorothy asked.

"They eventually burnt themselves out. Weather is natural, and just like anything natural, it has a certain lifespan. Nothing is forever."

"Tell that to Riya Lennox..."

"Hm?"

Dorothy shook her head to dismiss the comment. She moved to her wingback chair and took a seat facing the fire. The seat was large enough for them to both fit, if they squeezed, and neither of them much minded squeezing with the other. Cora put an arm around Dorothy and guided her head down to her shoulder. Dorothy allowed herself to be cradled, eyes locked on the fire.

"How are the girls?" Dorothy asked.

"Being treated as queens, naturally. The Keepings rented Florence a suite at the Grosvenor, all expenses paid, and every spa treatment requested. She will be living better than the King for the next month."

"I'm not sure that makes up for slapping her the way I did." Dorothy flexed her hand as if it still hurt, days later.

"She told you to do that. It was necessary to create more copies, to protect her." She kissed the top of Dorothy's head. "I wish we had taken turns just so you wouldn't have to bear the guilt alone."

"No. It was my idea. It should have been me. The others...?"

"The Keepings offered a Grosvenor suite to Mabel, but she refused. She just asked for some rest in her own bed. She doesn't think she did anything worthy of praise.

"Honour is still hard at work. She feels responsible for the weather, so she's using her weather manipulation powers to prevent flooding in areas the city might otherwise neglect. That's one reason I love working with these women. We all came from privilege, but they've fought and scrapped for everything they ever had. Most of them came from extreme poverty. They've lived in a part of London we've never seen. We had a huge blind spot, and they've forced us to address it."

"A very good point."

"Mm, thank you. I wanted you to be in a good mood before I told you about Edith."

Dorothy lifted her head. "What about her?"

Cora sighed and refused to meet Dorothy's gaze. "She was very, very weakened by the amount of healing energy she put out. Cecil says it almost killed her. Fortunately she seems to be recovering, but it was touch and go immediately after the event. He's livid about 'his girl' being used in that way."

"Oh, bugger him," Dorothy snapped. "You and the Keepings also had apprentices in the mix. Besides, we're all a singular group. The Mnemosyne Society is a whole, no matter who is apprenticing in what household."

"He sees it differently. He believes you and Trafalgar use the rest of us like tools."

"That's not true!" She remembered Cora's brutal honesty from before. "God, is it true?"

Cora shook her head. "No. You take command, you give orders, but you respect us all. Honestly we need someone to take command or else nothing would get done. But Cecil is adamant that when the next crisis arrives, you and Trafalgar will pick and choose which apprentice to sacrifice, and since his group is the most unpredictable..."

"Hogwash," Dorothy snorted.

"He's decided to make it impossible. By removing himself from the equation."

Dorothy went still. "And what does he mean by that?"

"Relocating. He intends to start a new branch of the Society located in another city. Leonard believes he'll choose Paris, but my money would be on New York. Easier for him to be a pompous ass there."

"Crumbs." She slumped against Cora's shoulder again. "Things fall apart, the center cannot hold."

"Perhaps it will be a good thing. The Inkwell was beginning to get a little crowded. And spreading our influence might help us in the future. If your use of magic erased Riya Lennox from the timeline, all that money she was funneling into our coffers will dry up, and soon we might not be able to travel wherever we want on a whim. It could be very beneficial to have someone stationed overseas if they're needed."

Dorothy stared at the fire. "And if they had already been in New York, we never would have gotten Edith here in time to deliver the cure. More people would have died. Trafalgar..."

Cora tucked a loose hair behind Dorothy's ear. "You would have thought of something. You always find the solution given the tools at your disposal."

"Yes, well. The best thing about doing something no one has ever done before is that it's impossible to prove you're doing it wrong. I'm terrified that one day in the future I'll discover I've made some terrible error and we didn't realize until it was too late to fix things."

"There's no one I would trust more to make those decisions. Someone has to step up when the time comes, and you never hesitate. No matter what dominoes you may set in motion, the simple truth is that you've saved the world more than you've harmed it. I will believe that no matter what chips may be yet to fall."

Dorothy managed a smile. "Thank you, Cora. You are so dear to me."

Cora kissed Dorothy between the eyebrows. "Any time, my love. We can't map the entire forest, so we can only take the path that looks best to us and deal with any consequences as they arise."

Dorothy nodded, trying to take comfort in the thought rather than focusing on the ominous implications it raised.

A door closed quietly upstairs. Dorothy lifted her head and looked toward the ceiling. "I thought all the other ladies had gone home."

"Hours ago," Cora confirmed.

"Dorothy?" Trafalgar called in a voice just loud enough to carry downstairs.

She got out of the chair and hurried to the door, arriving at the foot of the stairs to see Trafalgar on the landing above. She was wrapped in a shawl which had been folded at the foot of the bed, clutching it closed around her throat.

"You should be in bed," Dorothy scolded. "Although I have to admit, you do look much improved since the last time I saw you."

"I feel much improved." Trafalgar started down the steps, making slow but steady progress. She spoke between each riser, pausing to catch her breath. "Violet was exhausted. I wanted to let her sleep. Didn't want to disturb her by tossing and turning."

"That's very considerate of you. But you should still be lying down. You can take my bed."

"We don't know if I have any lingering illness, or if it could pass to Beatrice."

"Beatrice is... she's... she's gone."

Trafalgar paused. "Gone?"

"It's quite a long story."

"And that is why I'm coming down."

She arrived at the bottom step. She was already taller than Dorothy but, with this platform, Dorothy had to tilt her chin up to meet her eye.

"It's very clear that much has happened since I lost consciousness. It's time I was brought into the loop." She gestured at the parlor door, where Cora had appeared. "Shall we begin?"

In a restaurant kitchen Covent Garden, a distracted chef reached across the flame of his stove to retrieve a knife. A scream died in his throat as his sleeve ignited, but panic gave way to confusion as he watched the flame dance across his skin without damaging it. He extended his arm into the fire and spread his fingers. The fire licked and twisted around his wrist but it felt the same as reaching into a pot of lukewarm water.

Not far away from the chef's discovery, a prostitute shoved away a john who had gotten too rough. He muttered a curse and advanced on her, and she responded by punching him as hard as she could. The man flew off his feet and hit the wall hard enough to crater the plaster, and his neck bent at an unnatural angle before he collapsed in a heap at the floor.

Confidence men plied their trade, as shocked as their victims at how easily the cards were manipulated. A woman locked out of her home, drenched by the rain and more than a little desperate, made a futile attempt to jump to the second-floor window, only to find herself inexplicably on the roof. A man walked home with his head down, so lost in his thoughts that he didn't realize the rain was falling everywhere but on him.

There were other stories, more people discovering latent powers or displaying ability without quite understanding what had happened. There would be more in the coming days. Many, many more.

Magic had come to London.

## CHAPTER THIRTEEN

CORA EXCUSED herself, understanding that this was a private moment between the two friends. Trafalgar took a seat on the divan while Dorothy remained standing, pacing in front of the fireplace as she explained the events of the past few days. Occasionally she would pause in the narrative to watch for a reaction or to allow comments, but Trafalgar remained stone-faced and silent throughout the recitation. Dorothy laid out the entire chain of events, starting from Trafalgar's collapse in the Threadneedle doorway, to the banshee, and ending with how she utilized their new recruits to lift the curse. She also made a tangent to explain Beatrice's disappearance.

When she finished, she stopped pacing and stood in front of Trafalgar to await judgement.

"We had an agreement," Trafalgar finally said, looking at the fire rather than at Dorothy.

"Circumstances changed," Dorothy said. "The curse couldn't be lifted."

"You barely tried."

"We didn't have *time* to try anything else. People were starting to die. It was only a matter of time before you or Violet succumbed. Our backs were against the wall."

Trafalgar ran a hand over her face. "We're always doing this, you and I. Throwing out the rule book to save each other."

"What rule book?" Dorothy said. "We don't need a book. The only rule is to do everything in your power to save the people you care about. That's what I did."

"And how far will you go, Dorothy? Eventually we will come up against something we can't stop. Like what happened with Desmond. If you'd had access to a, a resurrection spell, would you have used it to bring him back to life and damn the consequences?"

Without hesitation, Dorothy said, "Absolutely I would." She stepped closer. "Are you saying you wouldn't? Had our positions been reversed, would you have let me die in order to keep a promise made to a woman we barely knew? A woman who could simply have been *lying* for whatever reason, just to make us serve her purpose."

"We saw what happened to Beatrice. Magic can be exhausted, and the results can be horrible."

"I couldn't stand by and watch this city slowly die when I knew it was within my power to save it. And in the future, I would make the same decision."

Trafalgar said, "What if these women had died in the attempt? Florence and Edith. Cora said that they're still recovering. Would you have traded their lives for mine?"

Dorothy sighed and started pacing again. "We have no loyalty to the future. It is permeable and constantly changing. Our only allegiance is to the present and the past. We make the world we want by making choices every day. Sometimes we make the wrong choices, and we have to live with that."

"Except when we don't. Except when we can wave our hands and summon a magical spell to undo the mistake. We take the easy way out, we never learn or lose or suffer, and we become weak. Fragile. It's precisely what Riya Lennox warned us about."

"Sodding bloody Riya Lennox," Dorothy sneered. "If it weren't for her, we wouldn't even be having this conversation. Magic would be just another tool at our disposal, like a weapon we purchased from Threnody. What about Ignacio Mata? We've been using his ability for years without questioning it."

Trafalgar said, "The difference is that now we know the cost of using magic. The more it's used, the more it gets abused, and eventually it goes away completely. We've dedicated our lives to unearthing great civilizations that came before ours. Kings and queens who ruled with mystical power, monsters and myths roamed the earth. And has it ever crossed your mind *how* these great societies crumbled? We talk about how magic was reawakened by the Great War, but we never asked how it went to sleep in the first place. We're dangerously close to joining those lost nations."

Dorothy was having a difficult time containing her anger. "I don't know if I'm more disturbed by the fact that you would have let me die from this illness or the fact you seem to be angry at me for saving your life."

"Of course I'm grateful to you for that," Trafalgar said softly. "And I will always do everything in my power to save you..."

"It sounds as if you would consider it a moral dilemma at best."

"Perhaps we shouldn't be discussing this right now. I still feel a bit lightheaded."

The tension faded from Dorothy's shoulders. "Right. You're obviously right." She came closer to the couch and offered her hand. She helped Trafalgar to her feet and put a hand between her shoulders as she helped her to the door. "We'll continue this discussion when you're feeling more settled. But please don't expect me to apologize for saving your life."

"Of course not." Trafalgar stopped and turned to face her. "Whatever happens, and however conflicted it might make me in the future, I will always be grateful to you for that. We owe each other our lives, Dorothy, and that unites us. Now and forever."

Dorothy brought Trafalgar's hand to her lips and kissed the knuckles. "I love you."

"And I, you."

They had just started up the stairs when the front door burst open. The rain, which until that point had faded to background noise, became a timpani. Cold, wet wind filled the foyer as Cora swept inside and pushed the door shut behind her. She tugged down the hood of her Mackintosh and looked into the parlor before she saw them on the stairs.

"Cora, what in the world..." Dorothy said.

Cora, breathless, pointed behind her. "People. Flying." She swallowed hard and tried to catch her breath. "People flying over the Thames. Some of the people watching said it's happening all over the city, different kinds of... of..."

"What?" Dorothy said.

"Magic," Trafalgar said. "First there was a wave of magic powerful enough to spread a fatal illness to everyone in London. The walls between worlds cracked. A few days later, a second wave of magic powerful enough to counteract the first. It was enough to cause the wall to shatter. We've broken down a barrier that was never meant to fall."

Dorothy said, "You mean I've broken it. This is my fault."

"We don't have the luxury of laying blame at this moment," Trafalgar said. "The first cracks opened during the Great War, we've only added to the damage."

"That was bad enough," Cora said. "It brought back creatures like the Minotaur, the snake woman we apparently fought in the Amazon, though we don't remember it because we twisted time. It enhanced the powers that Beatrice, the Virago, the Elephants were all born with. This time it seems to have worked much faster than it did the last time."

Cora said, "The War was like turning on the tap. I think this time we've destroyed the dam. We let in a flood. People flying over the Thames is just the first symptom. Something out there much worse is waiting to be known."

"Then let's go find it." Dorothy turned to Trafalgar. "Go back upstairs.

Rest. Don't rush your recovery. We need you back in fighting shape for whatever is out there."

Trafalgar looked as if she wanted to argue but knew there was no point in it. "Be careful."

"If I must." She pecked Trafalgar's cheek and went back down to join Cora in the foyer. She took her own raincoat from the closet along with a cap. "Do we know where the rest of the Mnemosyne Society is at the moment?"

"Agnes and Leonard are in Suffolk, but the majority of their apprentices are still here. Cecil is pouting and might not answer a summons even if we sent one. Some of his girls might. And my apprentices are at my estate."

"Then we'll go to your estate rather than moving them to the Inkwell in this weather."

As they went to the door, Trafalgar called out again, "Be careful, Dorothy!"

"You said that already," Dorothy chided her playfully.

"Maybe you'll be less likely to disregard it if I repeat myself enough times."

Dorothy smiled and nodded to her, then followed Cora back out into the rain.

**MAGICAL LONDON!**
Dorothy grimaced at the headline across the top page and put the newspaper down. She'd spent the evening at Cora's house as they got in touch with various contacts across London to learn the scope of what they were up against. It seemed the newspaper had the same sources, for much of the information was the same they'd heard over the phone. Women who were impervious to bullets, people who lost arms and legs only to have a new limb grow back in its place, flying men, women with the power of persuasion. The newspaper found people who had been physically transformed by the storm. They became lean, or robust, their blemishes faded or their skin turned to marble. Every street in London was a sideshow now, every doorway leading to some new freak or curiosity.

The newspaper speculated the illness had been a precursor to this "awakening of magical talents in the populace." The writer mentioned he had also gained a power, but declined to spell out what exactly it was. "Perhaps those so gleefully displaying their new abilities will wish they had done the same," he concluded, "for who knows when a secret power could come in very handy?"

Dorothy had read the article in Cora's breakfast nook. Dorothy loved Cora's house. It was large enough to accommodate her twelve apprentices, but the small rooms gave it a cozy feel. The kitchen was painted a robin's-egg blue which, as the storm had dissipated overnight, glowed brightly in the early morning sunshine.

She finished reading the article just as Cora came downstairs. Her hair was down, showing off much more silver than her usual updo revealed. She hadn't officially been to bed, only laid down for an hour or two so she could rise again refreshed. Dorothy greeted her with a nod and held up the newspaper, tapped the article with her finger.

"Word is out. The *Times* is suggesting people keep their powers under wraps for the time being."

"Fantastic," Cora grunted. "It was already going to be difficult to learn the scope of this thing. Now we have to wonder how many people aren't talking about how they were affected."

Two of Cora's apprentices came into the room, and it took Dorothy a moment to place them. The gamine young thing with the surprisingly large eyes and center-parted red hair was Susan McAlister, who could speak with plants. Her arm was hooked around the elbow of a dark-haired pale girl whom Dorothy had never seen smile: Myra Halfpenny, who could breathe underwater. Both girls were young enough to look like Cora's daughters, or perhaps students who had elected to visit their professor for breakfast before class.

"Morning, Miss Hyde," Susan said. "So glad the weather's cleared up, aren't you?"

"Yes, Susan. Say good morning to Lady Boone."

Susan pivoted. "My apologies, Lady Boone. A lovely morning to you."

Dorothy smiled and nodded to her.

"Anything to report?" Cora asked.

"No one is talking." Myra's voice was like a stone cracking against wood; flat, and completely without emotion. "I wouldn't talk, either. Not to us. Not to anyone. I didn't talk. Not until Miss Keaton came along."

Cora said, "That's what I was concerned about. People can see the risk of exploitation on their own, they'll make the decision to hide their powers. The newspaper will only inspire more people to do the same. And if I can make a confession, I'm not even certain what we hope to achieve. If the walls are broken down, if magic has flooded in, we can't put it back in. London is forever changed due to our actions."

"We may not be able to fix it," Dorothy admitted, "but it's my sincere hope that we can somehow contain it. Absolute power corrupts absolutely. There are hundreds of very bad people out there who just gained incredible abilities. I shudder to think what they will do with it."

Susan said, "So we're like constables? Keeping tabs on who can do what, and making sure they don't, you know, steal the crown or something?"

"For lack of a better term, yes," Dorothy said. "Our current police force will have no idea how to cope with a new class of magical criminals. We are better equipped, so it falls upon us to do what must be done. And we have to move quickly. Right now people are still in shock, uncertain about what's happened to them. It won't be long before they accept their new powers."

Susan said, "It took me a long time to figure out I could talk with plants. Even then, it didn't seem like I could do very much with it until Miss Keaton found me. I could tell a whole wall of flowers to let out their pollen in a tiny room. Everyone would run for fresh air and I'd be left alone to do whatever I wanted. There are others who have more obvious criminal abilities."

Myra said, "Walking through walls. Enhanced strength. Illusion and shapeshifting and stretching like rubber bands..."

Dorothy said, "Imagine every criminal in London waking up this morning and discovering they have powers like that."

"It will be anarchy," Cora said.

"Coppers never knew what to do with us," Susan said. "I overheard one of them say there wasn't even no point in locking us up, 'cause if we couldn't break ourselves out, we had friends who could do it for us."

"Right. Best eat up, girls. It would seem we have a long day ahead of us. If not a long week... months..."

Dorothy raised an eyebrow in agreement. They were fortunate the Mnemosyne Society had experienced its recent growth spurt. Even now, they would be stretched very thin, going up against an enemy they couldn't even begin to predict.

They were going to need as much help as they could find.

## CHAPTER FOURTEEN

TRAFALGAR WOKE up with a clear head, a normal temperature, and a woman spooning her. She initially believed it was Dorothy or Beatrice, as they were the only women she'd ever slept with, but her brain fog cleared and she remembered Violet. She rolled over without opening her eyes and pulled Violet closer. She used the excuse that she was only checking the other woman's temperature and pressed a kiss to her forehead. Violet murmured in her sleep, and then her hand squeezed Trafalgar's hip, and then her whole body tensed.

"Good morning," Trafalgar said.

Violet lifted her head, eyes wide and not quite focusing. She blinked. She blinked again. Then she wet her lips with her tongue and shrunk back.

"I... I-I'm sorry..."

"For what? I'm the one who kissed you."

Violet stared, blushing behind her freckles. "You... were. You did? You kissed me?"

"On the forehead."

"Oh."

Violet ducked her chin and looked past Trafalgar, examining the bedroom. Trafalgar took the opportunity to admire the shape of her cheek and the regal line of her nose. Though she was fair of complexion and hair, her eyes were dark chocolate. Her bottom lip was full, the upper lip a delicate bow, and it was all she could do to keep from brushing her thumb across it.

"My head is very foggy," Violet admitted. "I think a great many things happened, but I can't be certain which were real and which were only fever dreams."

"I think it would be smart to think the good things were real, while the bad can be attributed to the illness."

Violet met Trafalgar's gaze again. "The good things were quite good. And I wouldn't want to make an awkward advance."

"I'm an unattached woman who invited you into her bed. How awkward could it really be?"

"Unattached," Violet repeated.

Trafalgar said, "Mm. Very recently, in fact. Due to interest from unexpected quarters."

Violet exhaled sharply and pressed her cheek into the pillow, most likely to hide her smile. Trafalgar cupped the back of her head and leaned closer. Violet lifted her head and their lips met. The kiss lasted less time than either of them would have liked, but they seemed to agree at the same time that they were still too weak to go further. Trafalgar kissed both of Violet's cheeks and then scooted away from her.

"We should get up... try walking around. See if we feel more human once we're on our feet."

"I don't suppose I could borrow something of yours..."

Trafalgar said, "You could, but you look closer to Dorothy's size. You might be more comfortable in something from her closet."

"Are you sure she wouldn't mind? I'm already imposing by making myself a guest in her home."

"Our home," Trafalgar corrected. "She has no say in who I invite as a guest. And no, I have no doubt she would offer you a change of clothes if she was here."

Violet said, "If she makes a fuss, I will lay the blame on you."

"It would be only fair," Trafalgar said with a smirk.

Violet sat up and put her feet on the floor, paused, and stood up to test the strength of her legs. She looked back at Trafalgar with a grin.

"How about that?"

"Astounding," Trafalgar said. "Truly a marvelous feat of human endurance."

"Shush," Violet scolded. "Dorothy's room is..."

Trafalgar said, "Top floor, on your right."

Violet nodded and left. Trafalgar got up and dressed, only realizing she had chosen a purple shirt when she was doing up the buttons. She paused and ran her fingers over the buttons with a smile before she left her room. Violet was coming downstairs in flowing white slacks and a white blouse with a wide collar. She paused when she saw Trafalgar's outfit.

"Is that... a violet shirt...?"

"I've always considered it to be purple," Trafalgar admitted, touching the collar, "but I believe you may be correct. Violet is a much prettier color."

Violet smiled and was about to say something when the doorbell rang. They both looked downstairs toward the front door.

"Wonder who that is," Violet said in a tone that implied she would be fine with never knowing the answer.

"Pray for good news," Trafalgar said as she started down.

The woman on the front step was a constable in full uniform, the bucket had riding low on her brow to the point where it nearly covered her eyes. She was vaguely familiar, but Trafalgar couldn't place her until she spoke.

"Miss Trafalgar. Elsie Bracken."

"Yes, I remember," Trafalgar said. She was the one who had been driving when Dorothy gave chase to Maud Keaton. There was an accident in which Dorothy was gravely injured, but Elsie helped get her home where she could recover. It had been a harrowing few weeks, and it wasn't surprising that she had all but forgotten the woman.

"You look well," Elsie said, then looked at Violet. "And... Lady Boone...?"

"Violet Rhys," Trafalgar corrected. "She's an associate of ours."

Elsie nodded. "A'course. Is Lady Boone available?"

"Not at the moment, but perhaps we can help you."

"I surely hope so. May I come inside?"

Trafalgar invited her in. Violet, either uncertain about her role at this moment or just going on instinct, took the constable's hat and coat to hang them up. Trafalgar led Elsie into the parlor.

"I assume this is concerning the bizarre events of the past few days."

Elsie sighed heavily and nodded. "Truly bizarre, yes, miss. None of us have been able to make much sense of it. First people were calling us at all hours asking us to look in on their loved ones, due to that awful sickness that sprung up out of nowhere. Then this storm almost put us at the bottom of the Thames. And when that cleared up, suddenly people were calling with the strangest reports you've ever heard."

"For instance?" Trafalgar prompted.

"A woman called to say she heard her neighbor plotting to kill his wife. But she heard it in her head, like a thought. A jeweler called to tell us his entire inventory had been cleared out, but no locks were busted. And the *flying people*. The airship captains calling to report folks zipping about in their flightpath. I remembered you and Lady Boone from our last encounter, and it seemed like if anyone had a chance of knowing what was going on, it would be you."

Elsie suddenly turned and looked at Violet.

"We've met. Haven't we?"

Violet touched her lips, a not-so-subtle attempt to cover her face. "I don't think so..."

"I'm all but certain," Elsie said. "Violet Rhys, you said...?"

Trafalgar cleared her throat. "Constable, Violet was once a member of the Forty Elephants. That is likely how you recognize her. But when she was given the opportunity to make amends and walk the straight and narrow, she took it. She gave up the life of crime and now uses her talents to make the world a safer place under the tutelage of the Mnemosyne Society."

Violet looked terrified. Elsie stared at her, mentally judging the situation, then twisted her lips and turned away from her.

"We never could figure out how to keep those Elephants in custody. If they're out here being willingly reformed, I don't see any reason to throw 'em in the lockup."

Violet let out a breath. "Thank you, miss."

"Stick to lawfulness. We have enough problems without adding to the list." She looked hopefully at Trafalgar. "Do you think you can lend a hand? I've already talked to the higher-ups. Considering this is a special occasion, they're willing to reluctantly name the Mnemosyne Society as deputies if it will help sort this all out."

"We'd have to officially discuss it, of course," Trafalgar said, "but I'm certain that Dorothy and the others intend to intervene regardless. Being deputized would just make things easier. I'm prepared to tentatively agree."

Elsie closed her eyes with relief. "Thank heavens." Her smile faded. "Oh. I assume Missus Rhys isn't the only Elephant who is now a member of your group."

"No," Trafalgar said. "We've recruited all the surviving ladies."

"So that means we just deputized over thirty known criminals..." She winced. "I suppose desperate times, desperate measures, all that. But perhaps, if they could stay as out-of-sight as possible..."

Violet said, "One of us can actually turn invisible..."

"I didn't need to hear that," Elsie said, rising to her feet, "so I'll pretend I didn't. I'll go before there's anything else I don't need to hear. Miss Trafalgar, I thank you. And I will be your point of contact for any future updates, given our existing relationship."

Trafalgar stood to escort Elsie to the door. "It will be a joy to work with you again, Constable Bracken. I look forward to it."

She retrieved her hat and coat, wished them good luck, and left.

As soon as the door was closed behind her, Violet said, "That wasn't your story to tell."

Trafalgar turned. "I apologize. It didn't look as if you were comfortable saying it yourself, and the truth would have come out eventually. I thought it was best to get it all out in the open."

"Perhaps. Probably, yes, I believe you're right. But I still wish you hadn't spoken up. Even though..." She grunted and shook her head. "Even though I'm grateful you saved me from having to say it myself. God, I don't know how I feel."

"You feel conflicted," Trafalgar said, "and that's okay. I owe you an apology for telling things you might have preferred to remain secret, and accept your gratitude for taking the pressure off in a very tense moment. Does that cover it?"

Violet smiled a little. "I think so, yes." She looked at her shoes. "Does it bother you? That I used to be a criminal?"

Trafalgar shrugged. "Trix used to be a thief. She met Dorothy while robbing this house. We've all done things we're less than proud of in the pursuit of living. Second chances are the only reason any of us are able to grow. Our mistakes make us who we are as much as our successes."

"Thank you."

Trafalgar stepped closer and cupped Violet's face. Violet tilted her head up and Trafalgar kissed her.

"There's also the delicate matter of... we may end up working at cross-purposes with Dorothy and the rest of the Society."

"How do you mean?"

Trafalgar pressed her lips together. "This outbreak. Dorothy and I agreed that the best course of action would be to keep magical use in check. She seems to have completely changed her opinion. We can fight against these newfound threats one by one, but I think the best course of action will be to find a way to quell it completely. If we can somehow reestablish the barriers between our world and the magical realm, or put the energy back to sleep, the world will return to normal."

Violet said, "So we'd all lose our abilities?"

"I honestly don't know. How would you feel about that?"

"My ability is to see things that are far away. I don't know if I'll need it when the only thing I want is right in front of me."

Trafalgar started to smile, but emotion got the better of her. She ducked her head and took Violet's hand. She waited a moment to be certain she could speak without her voice quavering.

"For now, we need to give the impression we're working toward the same goal. To do that, I need to figure out where Dorothy spent the night so we can inform her of our new status with law enforcement."

"Oh." Violet closed her eyes. She looked like she was trying to recall a complicated line of poetry. "She's... in a very blue room. Sunlight. Susan and Myra are there. Miss Hyde." She opened her eyes and smiled victoriously. "She's having breakfast at Miss Hyde's home."

Trafalgar shook her head in amazement. "Your ability truly is astounding."

"It's nothing. It's just looking."

Trafalgar shook her head. "You are a wonder even without the Sight."

Violet affected a stern expression, her posture rigid. "You seem to have the power to make me blush, Trafalgar, and I'll thank you to keep it under wraps when we're in mixed company. A lady has a reputation to maintain."

"I make no promises, Violet."

"Good," Violet said, dropping the act with a laugh as Trafalgar opened the door to lead her out into the morning.

## CHAPTER FIFTEEN

THEIR TRIP hit its first snag as soon as they got into the sedan. Trafalgar got behind the wheel, glanced into the backseat, then immediately looked again. She examined the leather seat carefully and, finding nothing, faced forward again. But she kept her hands on the steering wheel and left the engine silent. Violet watched her, looked in the back as well, and then looked at Trafalgar with concern.

"Is something wrong?"

"Perhaps," Trafalgar said. "Although I don't know if I've picked up some of Dorothy's intuition or if you're just losing your touch."

"My touch...?"

"Not you," Trafalgar said, then looked over her shoulder. "Which is it, Miss Sever?"

"Six of one."

Violet yelped and scooted forward to the front of her seat, twisting to see who had spoken. The voice came from the back, but she could clearly see it was empty.

Trafalgar said, "Violet Rhys, allow me to introduce the most troublesome member of the Mnemosyne Society, Ivy Sever."

"Charmed, I'm sure," Ivy said with exaggerated poshness.

"I-I remember." She averted her gaze. "What we did to you was cruel."

Ivy was quiet for a moment. Finally, she said, "That was Maud Keaton's doing. Besides, she didn't know what would happen."

"She suspected there was a reason Lady Boone hadn't offered you the cure. She elected to ignore it, and none of us pushed her on it."

"Sure. Okay. It didn't seem like the sort of organization where speaking up would be rewarded. Let's just forget it, yeah?"

Violet said, "So long as you know you have my deepest apologies."

"So acknowledged." Given the tension in her voice, Ivy was probably grateful that neither of them could see her face. "Can we move on, please? Where are we going?"

Trafalgar said, "Forget that. Where have you *been*? No one's heard from you since the Forty Elephants disbanded."

"Things to do. Mind to get right. Didn't need you lot pestering me about my feelings. But now we've got bigger problems. I assume it's all hands on deck for the Society, yeah? London's full of magic and people are flying all over the place. We know what caused it?"

"Yes. Dorothy."

Ivy snorted. "That figures. So is there a plan yet or are we just winging it?"

Trafalgar didn't say anything, debate raging on her features. "Our... goal may not be the same as Dorothy's. I believe she's willing to accept the current situation as the status quo. She seems to think this is just an evolutionary leap. I believe we can, and should, try to fix things. We want to end magic, if it is at all possible. The world will be better off if humanity stands on its own two feet without relying on tricks or special powers."

"Huh." Ivy chuckled under her breath. "Well, all right then. I s'pose I'll just tag along and see which one of you seems to be on the right path. But I won't tell her you're trying to undermine her."

"Thank you."

"Unless it benefits me, of course."

Trafalgar sighed and looked at Violet, shook her head, and finally started the car. "Just lovely to have you back, Miss Sever. You were truly missed. When are you leaving again?"

Ivy laughed as the car pulled away from the curb.

Trafalgar, Violet, and Ivy arrived at Cora's house just as the group was preparing to leave for the Inkwell. Dorothy wished to address the entire Society, and the tavern's courtyard was the only place large enough for everyone to gather. Dorothy welcomed Ivy back with genuine gladness. She held no grudge for the actions Ivy had taken on the part of Maud Keaton. A part of her was concerned with the length of Ivy's absence, and the fact that no one had seen hide nor hair of Maud or the Elephants who chose to leave London with her. The last report had them boarding an airship called *Ninox*, bound for France, but every passenger aboard vanished before they arrived. It was precisely the sort of locked-room mystery an invisible assassin might pull off, but they had far more pressing concerns at the moment.

The women in the courtyard gathered in their own cliques, each cluster representing their mentor. Agnes and Leonard, who had returned that morning from Suffolk, were along the northern wall, with Cora at the south. Cecil and his women were against the Inkwell's wall, as far away from Dorothy as they could get. Dorothy knew this wasn't an accident on his part, and the stern looks she received from the women indicated they shared his opinion of her. She had no defense. She had used their friends as tools, and she refused to apologize for that.

She put that out of her mind as she stood in front of the group. Trafalgar was at her left, and Ivy had slipped away into the crowd after refusing to put on some clothes so they could keep track of her. Dorothy lifted one hand, snapping her fingers until the chatter died down.

"Welcome, Mnemosyne Society. Clearly you all know why you're here today. The people of London have been changed, and we are to blame. There will be many people who are frightened and confused by what's happened, just as you were when your powers first manifested. There will be others who see their new abilities as an opportunity to cause mayhem. The responsibility for these people falls to us. Not just because we opened the door to magic, but because all of you have been in the same place they find themselves now. Scared. Or too intrigued by the potential to think clearly about their actions. People will be hurt if we don't intervene.

"As glad as it makes me to see you standing with your respective groups, the time has come for that to end. Your mentors will obviously still be there for you, if you need them, but this problem will require all of us working as a group. There are no more apprentices, no more assignments. You will be asked to assist with missions as needed, and you will work with whomever you choose.

"Zilla Beverly, you are no longer the responsibility of the Keepings. You are a member of this Society in full standing." She chose another woman at random. "Angel Tuffin. You are obviously more than welcome to continue working with Cora, as Trafalgar and Beatrice choose to work closely with me. But the choice will be yours, and you will work together as equals."

Before she could choose a member of Cecil's group, one of them held up her hand. Dorothy recognized her as Ann Stead. "We choose to remain with Mister Dubourne. I speak for all of us." The women around her nodded their agreement.

Dorothy worked her jaw in an effort to keep her expression neutral. "Excellent. I'm glad to see you've developed such a strong camaraderie. But for now, for this particular mission, we are one group with one purpose. We will find those affected by the magical awakening and we will lend them our aid, or subdue them as necessary."

She thought she noticed a look pass between Trafalgar and Violet, but she dismissed it as nerves and paranoia.

Charlotte Fleming, one of Cecil's group, spoke without raising her hand. "A group of equals sounds good, but someone's got to be giving the orders. You may have been running the show when it was just a handful of you, but if we're really going to be equals, shouldn't we have a say in who leads us? Who's going to be in charge?"

Cora said, "Just for the sake of simplicity, does everyone agree to allow their mentor to cast the deciding vote?"

Heads nodded all around. The groups began to whisper amongst themselves, some debating longer than others.

Agnes was the first to speak up. "Dorothy and Trafalgar."

Leonard nodded, adding, "This entire group was their idea. Time and again, they've taken the weight of the Society on their shoulders, but they strive for diplomacy. They aren't only the proper choice, they are the smart choice."

"And if I may remind you all," Cora said, "these two women are a big part of why you're standing here as free women rather than locked up, drugged, or used as experiments. They faced you as enemies but treated you like allies. That should bear weight. I also vote for Dorothy."

Dorothy cleared her throat. "Not that it matters, but I was going to vote for the Keepings."

"I second that vote," Cecil said quickly. "Two for Boone, two for the geezers. That's a tie."

Leonard said, "Agnes and I both chose Dorothy."

One of Cecil's women, Eveline Barrington, said, "You're being elected as a pair, and you'd be in charge as a pair. So you only get a single vote. It's the same reason Trafalgar can't vote for Lady Boone."

"Looks like it's a good thing I decided to come back today."

Ivy's voice seemed to come from the center of the courtyard, but there was no evidence to reveal exactly where she was standing.

"This should be interesting," Agnes said, crossing her arms over her chest. "She hates all of us."

"Nothing interesting about it," Ivy said. "You all know that I turned on Dorothy not long ago. Hell, some of you were even part of that bullshit. But the fact is, me and most of everyone here would be dead without Lady Boone. She makes the plans. She forgives. She offers second chances. Hell, she's got us this far. If we have to officially elect her, then let's get it over with. There's a big city out there that needs a lot of help, and we can't stand around all day playing who gets to be queen."

Cora said, "Agreed. I think this vote was necessary, but we've spent enough time on it. If anyone has any true objections to Dorothy being in charge, now would be the time to air your grievance."

Though no one looked directly at Cecil or his group, it was obvious everyone expected dissent to come from them. For a long, tense moment, no one said anything. Finally, Cecil smiled and gestured at Dorothy in a move that could almost be called a bow.

"Long live the queen."

"Fabulous," Dorothy said.

Despite being the de facto leader since the Society was formed, it still felt as if something monumental had been bestowed upon her. In a way, it had. Being in charge of a half dozen people she knew was much different than being the leader of forty people. A third of whom apparently hated her. It would be fine. She would win them over in time, just as she had won over Trafalgar. She smoothed her hands down the front of her vest to give herself a moment before she spoke again.

"Before arriving this morning, Trafalgar informed me that we've been deputized. That means we will be working as emissaries of the local police force. This does not give anyone the authority to break the law, but we will be able to place people under arrest should the need arise. We'll be canvassing the city in groups of two. Everyone can choose their own partner. It should be someone you trust to watch your back even in the most dire circumstances."

"What exactly are we even looking for?" Isabella Stannard asked. "Are we knocking on doors, asking people to show us their powers?"

"We'll be patrolling," Dorothy said. "Watching for signs of trouble. The people we're concerned about won't be able to control themselves."

"How about that?" Emily Tripp said, smirking. "We used to run from bobbies, now we're the ones in charge. Kind of a nice feeling."

"Do your best to find a partner from another group. We all need to learn how to work together now. This is a trial by fire, but I think it will be a good chance to learn about one another. I'm not entirely certain we have an even number of people. If there are stragglers—"

"I'll make an extra to make up the difference," Florence said.

Dorothy stared at her, skeptical. "Florence, that is a very kind offer, but after what you've just been through—"

Florence held up a hand. "It's forgotten. Everything came out peachy in the end, and I'm glad to suffer a little soreness if it means helping a lot of other people. Just let me know where you need me, and I... *we* will be there."

"In that case, I thank you."

The crowd began pairing up. Dorothy watched and felt the tension easing from her shoulders. She expected arguments, disagreements, petty nonsense between the groups, but no one raised a voice or raised a fuss. "Well," she muttered to where Trafalgar had been standing, "it would seem everyone already has a fair idea who..."

She realized she was standing alone, but she didn't have to look far to find Trafalgar. She had only taken a few steps, and was already caught up in a discussion with Violet Rhys.

"Who their partner is," Dorothy finished, raising an eyebrow.

Trafalgar came back over. "Violet has some ideas about where ne'er-dowells might choose to exploit their newfound powers."

Dorothy nodded. "By all means, follow the lead. I'm sure I'll find someone to partner with."

Trafalgar seemed surprised. "Hm? Oh! You expected us to... that's, ah~"

"Trafalgar, relax," Dorothy said with a laugh. "It's a good lead, and you seem to have developed quite a rapport with Miss Rhys in the short time you've known one another. I would never stand in the way of such a promising relationship."

"I don't know what you're talking about."

Dorothy examined Trafalgar's face. "You mentioned the prospects of starting a romance with her. Am I misreading~"

"No, no." Trafalgar looked back at Violet, who looked away to avoid being caught staring. "But I don't think either of us would like it to be common knowledge. Perhaps it would be best if I joined you."

"Absolutely not. Go. I'll find someone to pair with." She squeezed Trafalgar's arm. "Go on. And try to have a little fun while you're working."

Trafalgar tried to fight a smile and failed. "Good luck."

She went back to Violet, and they left together.

"Boone."

Dorothy jumped and turned toward her best approximation of where the voice had come from. "Ivy. Lovely to have you back. I'm sure you spent your time away reflecting on your life choices and vowing to do better in the future."

"You can believe that if you'd like, sure," Ivy said. "You know I don't play well with others. Some of these bitches are the ones who lied to me, tricked me, gave me false hope. I'm willing to forgive that, but not yet. As for you or Trafalgar, well, that's... I don't feel comfortable asking you to trust me, either. So that's a long-winded way of saying that I'm not teaming up with no one. But I'll be out there representing the Society to the best of my abilities. Is that enough for you?"

Dorothy extended her hand to thin air. "You're literally giving as much as you possibly can, Ivy. How can I expect more?"

A ghostly hand gripped hers.

"Whenever you're ready to give more, we'll consider ourselves fortunate to have you."

"Okay," Ivy said. "All right. Well..."

The hand vanished, and Dorothy felt the invisible assassin depart.

The courtyard slowly began to empty out as each pair to follow their own leads. Dorothy remained by the gate and tried to gauge everyone's mood. The women who had apprenticed with Cora and the Keepings seemed friendly or indifferent toward her, but Cecil's crew seemed outright cold when they passed. She noticed these women had paired exclusively with each other with no crossing over. Troubling.

Cora was the last to leave. She had partnered with the sprite, Sadie Halladay. "Looks like you're the odd one out, Lady Boone. You're free to join up with us. We're going to King George Hospital to see if anyone has confused their newfound powers with an onset of an illness."

"Good thinking," Dorothy said. "And no, while I appreciate the offer, I believe it would be best if we stick to pairs. I can remain here to serve as a general for the troops, should anyone require guidance."

Cora raised an eyebrow. "This leadership thing has already gone straight to your head, hasn't it?"

"I don't know what you're talking about. And I expect you to address me as 'ma'am' when we're in the trenches."

"I thought I was the only one who called you 'ma'am'."

Dorothy recognized the voice but was still confused as she turned around. She didn't dare believe it, especially after spending the morning with a group of magical women who could cast illusions, create false memories, and shapeshift at will. The woman walking toward her looked fragile and wan, her skin smeared with streaks of dirt. Her dark hair hung loose, much longer than Dorothy was used to seeing it, and she wore only a mud-streaked undershirt with a pair of white slacks. She was barefoot but seemed unbothered by the street stones as she closed the distance between them.

It was Cora who broke the silence, and confirmed that Dorothy wasn't hallucinating. "Beatrice? Good lord, you're awake."

"Maybe not entirely up to snuff yet, but it would seem I am. Hello, Miss Hyde." Her eyes shifted to Dorothy, and her expression softened. She cupped Dorothy's face with both hands. "Hello, Lady Boone. Sorry to be so late to work. I overslept."

Dorothy blinked and both her eyes spilled tears down her cheeks. "How many times do I have to tell you that you're fired?"

"I'll let you know, Lady Boone."

Then she leaned in and kissed her, and Dorothy allowed herself to sob as she wrapped her arms around the woman she'd thought was lost forever.

When the kiss ended, Dorothy embraced her, buried her face against Beatrice's shoulder, and breathed in her scent. It was the smell of dirt and grass, sweat, and blood.

"Welcome home, Trix. Welcome back."

## CHAPTER SIXTEEN

TRAFALGAR AND Violet elected to walk to the hospital, which would make it easier for them to spot unusual behavior on the street. They passed the time by talking. Trafalgar told the story about how she was brought from Ethiopia by men who planned to use her body as a vessel for some kind of ceremony, but she managed to overtake them. She was called "Tall Girl" then, but a misunderstanding led to her becoming identified as Trafalgar. She liked the name as well as any other, so it stuck.

"It suits you," Violet said. "I never thought of it as a person's name, or what a person with that name might be like, but... yes. You are very much a Trafalgar."

"And I doubt there are many people who could survive being named after a flower, and yet here you stand."

Violet laughed while also rolling her eyes. "It's not the name I would have chosen for myself, but we each take the lots we're given in life. My sisters were Rose, Poppy, and Daisy. I suppose it could have been worse and I'd have to suffer under a name like... Hyacinth."

"Hyacinth Rhys has a certain charm to it, though," Trafalgar argued. "It's musical."

"Mm, perhaps."

Violet uncrossed her arms and walked with them awkwardly at her sides for a moment, then reached out to slip one around Trafalgar's elbow. Trafalgar smiled and pulled her closer.

"So we're just two unfortunate souls shackled with names we didn't choose, but which we've made our own."

They continued on, arm-in-arm. Trafalgar didn't feel a need to fill the silence, but she did have questions, and it seemed as if they might not get another opportunity for a conversation.

"May I ask about... well, I suppose I want to know how your story began. Discovering you had powers, joining up with Maud Keaton. Forgive me for saying, but you hardly seem like the type to choose a life of crime and join the Forty Elephants."

Violet took a deep breath. "Ah..."

"If you would prefer not to tell me~"

"No. No. Anyone else, yes, they'd be out of luck and a bit sore in the jaw for even asking. But I'll tell you."

Trafalgar patted Violet's hand with hers, a silent show of gratitude, but she remained silent so Violet could steel herself for what she had to say.

"I spent my entire life putting a brick wall around myself. There were things I wanted, that no one would allow me to do. So I hid and I made myself the person my mother wanted me to be. I was her perfect child who wanted to wear her hair long. Who craved the attention of boys and wanted nothing more than to be a good homemaker. I was going to be wed to the first man who treated me kindly, although I did hope to find one who shared my shameful desires. Well. Not shared..."

"I understand."

Violet nodded and scanned the street ahead of them. "One day, a boy from a neighboring farm went missing. His family was utterly distraught, as you would expect. We all gathered to search for him. We were all desperate with fright by sundown. So I closed my eyes and concentrated as hard as I could. I knew he had fallen down a small hill at the far reaches of their property. He was unconscious and his leg was broken. His father ran out and found him. My reward was to be called a witch, accused of sorcery and worshipping the Devil. My mother banished me from the house to protect my sisters from my influence. She only let me pack a bag because it meant fewer tainted things for her to burn once I was gone.

"So I came to London, where I was finally free to do whatever I wanted. I found a woman who wanted to take me to bed. She gave me alcohol for the first time, and I woke up without my bag or the small amount of money I'd managed to grab when I left home. It wasn't much, but it was mine. And I had nothing. I didn't even get to fuck the woman before she robbed me!"

Trafalgar smiled, though she didn't find any part of the story humorous.

"I made a sign. Lost Treasures Found. Ten P. Then I waited. I found watches, eyeglasses, pens, all sorts of tosh. I just sat on the street and told people where to look. They would go away and I'd either never see them again, or they'd come back to accuse me of stealing it from them in the first place. I had to leg it more than once to avoid a beating."

Trafalgar said, "I'm sorry."

Violet shrugged and looked down, watching their feet on the pavement. "One day, Maud Keaton showed up. She said she had an experiment for me. She showed me a locket, nothing special, and asked me to remember it. Paid me a whole pound. So I remembered. She came back a week later and asked me where it was. I told her. Top drawer of a bureau in a house not far from where we were. 'Can you show me?' she said. So I took her right to it, pointed to the window. She told me I'd done an excellent job and gave me five pounds. Offered me a place to stay, steady employment if I wanted it. All I had to do was go through jewelry shops, stores, banks, and keep an eye on people. Then later on, I'd tell Maud that a fur coat went to this house, that one had some shiny new pearls, and the man of that house left the bank with a big withdrawal."

"And then the others would rob the houses."

"Yes. I never went on those jobs. Sadie, Alma, Mayra... those were the ones who did the smashy-grab. I'm not using that as an excuse. I know I'm just as culpable for those crimes as the others. I don't want you to think of me as someone who was crawling in windows and sneaking around in the dark."

"It wouldn't make me think less of you. I think you're a remarkable woman, Miss Rhys, and one trait of remarkable women is that they frequently suffer tragedies that would topple a lesser person. You are not the awful things that happened to you. They did not make you who you are. They did everything in their power to crush you, and yet, here you stand. If anything it makes me more impressed by you. Thank you for trusting me with your story."

"Thank you for telling me yours."

They continued on for several blocks and had nearly arrived at the hospital when their attention was grabbed by a scuffle in an alleyway. Trafalgar hurried to investigate and Violet followed. They arrived in time to see one man punching another in the stomach. The victim doubled over but brought his hand up, swept it in front of the attacker's face, and an arc of blood flew to splatter against the brick. The puncher fell backward and clutched his now red throat, while his erstwhile victim straightened up and looked down. His right arm now ended in a silver, blood-spotted blade. He twitched his elbow and the blade transformed into a normal hand.

"Stand where you are!" Trafalgar shouted. "Do not move!"

He looked at her and smiled evilly as he considered whether he should fight or flee. He decided on the latter and took off at a run, quickly disappearing around a corner.

"Damn." Trafalgar started to follow, but Violet put a hand on her arm. "Stay here and take care of him. He can still be saved. I'll catch our silverblade."

"He's got a head start. He's bound to know these alleyways like~"

Violet closed her eyes. "He turned right, continued along for fifty paces, turned left. He jumped onto a ladder and..." She rocked her head from side to side as she waited for him to climb. "Now he's on the roof running easterly."

"Be careful."

Violet nodded. "You too."

Trafalgar caught her before she could run off and pulled her close, pressing a kiss to her lips. Violet gasped and slipped an arm around Trafalgar's waist, allowing herself to be dipped backward briefly before she was returned to her feet.

"Make haste, Miss Rhys."

Violet's face was flushed and she turned away with a chuckle. Trafalgar turned to the victim and winced as she saw his bloody hand.

"Sorry about that, chap. You probably wish we'd been a bit hastier in lending you a hand."

She reached for him, but he slapped her away. Before she could react, he slammed himself into the wall and exploded into a wave of water. Trafalgar jumped back to avoid being splashed. The water pooled around itself and became a clear, shining slug that darted toward the mouth of the alley.

"I suppose it's a good sign that I can still be surprised by things like this," she muttered with a smile. She shook her head in disbelief, then decided to try catching up with Violet to lend her assistance.


Cora and Dorothy helped Beatrice into the Inkwell, while Sadie dashed to Threadneedle to get her a clean outfit. By the time she returned, they had gotten Beatrice into a booth and Cora was in the middle of pouring a large glass of water. Beatrice seemed to have exhausted all of her energy just to get to the tavern and slumped against Dorothy's side, eyes closed. They were holding hands so tightly that Dorothy was starting to lose the feeling in her fingers, but it was worth it to feel Beatrice squeezing back.

"I woke underground." Beatrice opened her eyes and accepted the glass from Cora. "Thank you. There was dirt in my mouth, my nose, eyes... it was terrifying. But I wasn't buried deep and it all fell away during my initial thrashing. The Dov was there. She explained what had happened to me. Apparently she expected my revival to take much longer, but there was what she described as a tsunami of powerful energy that washed over all of London. She said that's what pushed me over the edge, made me wake up."

Cora had also brought a pitcher and a towel. Dorothy wrapped the towel around two fingers, wet it, and began gently scrubbing the dirt from Beatrice's face and neck.

"You don't remember anything since your collapse?"

Beatrice shook her head. "Vague impressions, I suppose. They could just be dreams of memories. The Dov told me I traveled on another plane and briefly used her as a vessel. I don't remember any of that. The last thing I know was being on the *Skylarker*, preparing to assault the Elephants house. So... did we win?"

Dorothy said yes at the same time Sadie said no. Everyone looked at her, and she shrugged. "You convinced our boss to run away, and a couple chose to go with her, and the rest of decided we might as well join up with you lot."

"You're an Elephant?" Beatrice said.

"Was," Sadie corrected. "Now I'm a full-fledged member of the Mnemosyne Society."

"You're..." Beatrice looked at Dorothy, who reluctantly shrugged and nodded. "Sounds like I missed a lot while I was laid out."

Cora said, "There will be plenty of time to fill you in about everything once you've rested. Truly rested. You may have recovered enough to regain consciousness, but any fool could see you're not up to your full potential yet. We've got more than enough people helping us out. You can take a few days before you try to join in the fight."

"I agree," Dorothy said. "And until we have a better idea of what you've been through, I don't want you to use any magic."

"That's a bit extreme," Beatrice said without much conviction.

Dorothy brushed some grime from Beatrice's cheek. "I will not bury you again, Beatrice Sek, even if it does heal you. So we're going to play it safe."

Beatrice looked at Dorothy with love and adoration. "I suppose there's no sense arguing with you, Lady Boone."

"It's about time you learned that lesson. Now, to more pressing questions... how did you know to find us here? Shouldn't you have gone to Threadneedle first?"

"That was where I assumed you would be," Beatrice said, "but the Dov told me there was a huge concentration of adept individuals gathered here. We both thought it was likely you'd be here. Though I never would have suspected you were at a gathering of Elephants. *Former* Elephants."

"They've proven to be invaluable to the group," Dorothy said.

Beatrice finished the water and Cora went to get her a refill. "So what are we facing?"

Dorothy explained the illness, their cure, and the consequences as succinctly as possible. Beatrice listened, eyes drifting shut from time to time but her head never lolling to indicate she was falling asleep.

"So everyone in London has magic now?" she asked when Dorothy finished.

"It can't be everyone," Dorothy said. "But it stands to reason that a great many people have some ability or another, yes. The Great War cracked the wall between our world and the realm of magic, and I believe our actions have just sent it crashing to the ground. I can't pretend I know what the consequences might be, and according to Riya Lennox, I've just signed humanity's death warrant. But I refuse to believe that. And I will never regret an action which not only healed Trafalgar but brought Trix back to me. We'll find a way to overcome this, just as we always have, because now all three of us are in the fight. There's no problem too big when the three of us are together."

Something crashed in the distance, as if to punctuate Dorothy's declaration. Sadie was the first one to reach the door, naturally, and she stepped outside. She tilted her head back and cupped a hand over her eyes to block the sun.

"I understand your friend there just went through an ordeal, but I don't think she's gonna have time to just sit and relax."

Cora hurried to join her. "What is it? What was that sound?"

"From the looks of it," Sadie said, "it seems as if a man taller than the clouds just got hit in the back by an airship. The ship is a smoking wreck but still flying, and I think the tall fellow is bleeding into the Thames. I'd say whatever bright idea you three wonders might have brewing, you better put it into motion right quick."

Dorothy looked at Beatrice, took a deep breath, and let it out slowly.

"Crumbs."

## CHAPTER SEVENTEEN

NIGHT HAD fallen by the time Trafalgar and Violet trudged back to Threadneedle Street, sore and utterly exhausted by the events of the day. Even for them, with their experience facing monsters and magic and ancient curses, they'd been caught unprepared for the sheer magnitude of how London had changed. Almost immediately after the man who could turn his arms into knives was apprehended and turned over to the constables, another man became so immense that an airship crashed into his back. They were on their way to try dealing with that when they were waylaid by a man who had melted into the street and couldn't figure out how to reconstitute himself.

There were so many that Trafalgar found it difficult to remember all of them. They blended together in her mind, even as strange as they all were.

"Do you find it odd that it's mostly men?" Violet asked.

"Not at all," Trafalgar said, trying to keep the weariness from her voice. "Any man given new power will immediately try to master it, see what he can gain from it, push the limits. The women, however... we remember what historically happens to women who have power. Witch trials and burning at the stake. We're wary enough to keep to ourselves in the face of uncertainty."

Violet said, "Mm," and put her head on Trafalgar's shoulder. "I'm exhausted."

"We're almost there. Would you like me to keep talking so you won't fall asleep?"

"No, that's not necessary. Although I do like the sound of your voice."

Trafalgar smiled and patted Violet's hand. "We're almost there," she said again.

They had just left a small group of other former Elephants who were on their way to patrol Piccadilly. Even though they were supposed to be working in pairs, they'd run into a couple of problems that required more people. "Teamwork is the goal, right?" Zilla Beverly said with a shrug, and Trafalgar agreed. As long as they operated as a team, they were more than welcome to improvise in the field.

Susan McAlister pointed out that they should work out shifts. She volunteered to stay on until morning while some of their group went home to get some sleep and start fresh in the morning

"It's a good idea," Trafalgar said. "The people who wait until nightfall to test out their new abilities will be the ones truly worth worrying about."

She reluctantly found herself volunteered as one of the people who would go home and rest. She didn't want to, but Susan argued that she and Violet were technically still recovering from the plague. She had to admit she was much more tired than she should have been. She thanked Susan for the suggestion but turned down the offer of taking a car the group had procured.

"The night air will do me good," she said. "I'll see you all in the morning."

Isabella and Helena were both Keepings girls, like Violet, and Trafalgar expected Violet to ride with them back to the boardinghouse. She was surprised when the car pulled away from the curb without her in it. She was even more surprised when she said goodbye to the remaining women and walked away, only to find Violet walking alongside her. She hadn't said anything at the time, but as they drew closer to the house, she needed to know.

"Violet... now that you're not ill, there's really no reason for you to spend the night at Threadneedle."

"I was hoping I would still be invited."

"Absolutely you are. But there's a dearth of beds. One wouldn't want to presume..."

Violet squeezed Trafalgar's arm. "One can think whatever one wants, Miss Trafalgar. Tell me if it's unwanted and I'll sleep on that divan I saw in the parlor."

"It's very much wanted, Violet."

The front windows of the Threadneedle house shone with an inviting golden light, and Trafalgar felt the weariness of the day settle on her shoulders as she escorted Violet inside. She scanned the front rooms but couldn't see anyone.

"Dorothy may have left the lights on to deter burglars. She could still be at the Inkwell."

"Lady Boone has retired to the bath," Beatrice said as she descended the stairs. She wore her standard uniform of black jacket, waistcoat, and button-down white blouse. She looked dreadfully thin, and her face was ashen, but the smile on her lips was the most beautiful thing in the world. "I would be happy to let her know we have guests."

Trafalgar moved without thinking, gliding up the stairs without taking her eyes off the vision before her. She reached out and Beatrice, smiling wider, also reached out her hand. She pressed their palms together, linked their fingers, and squeezed.

"Hello, Miss Trafalgar."

"Trix..."

"No tricks."

Trafalgar wrapped Beatrice in a hug. Beatrice was on a higher step, so it was easy for Trafalgar to press her face against the shoulder of her uniform jacket. She smelled like earth and water but, much more importantly, she returned the embrace and chuckled softly before kissing Trafalgar's temple.

"Easy," Beatrice said. "I'm not completely recovered. From what Dorothy told me, neither are you."

"Right, sorry. My god." She stepped back and cupped Beatrice's cheek. "How?"

"We can discuss it in the morning. You've had a busy day, and you didn't even have to fight the giant man."

Trafalgar said, "Who took care of him?"

"Angel, who is apparently very strong and telepathic, and Eveline Barrington, who is a sharpshooter. It was impressive to see."

"Yes, it would seem it's a day full of remarkable sights. Oh!" She turned and gestured. "Violet Rhys, this is Beatrice Sek. Beatrice, Violet."

Beatrice nodded. "Pleasure."

"Same. I've heard a lot about you. Glad to see you're well."

"Mm." She let her eyes travel up and down the other woman before she turned back to Trafalgar. "I'll let you rest. I was just coming down to get some extra blankets." She hugged Trafalgar again, and this time turned her head to whisper in her ear. "Dorothy told me. I approve very much. Have fun."

Trafalgar kissed Beatrice's cheek. "I thought you were fired."

"Dorothy thought the same. But I like what I do far too much to let myself be fired."

Trafalgar grinned and a tear slipped down her cheek. "It is wonderful to see you again, Beatrice."

"Sleep well. We'll have more than enough time to catch up in the morning."

Beatrice continued down the stairs and wished Violet a good night, then continued to the kitchen. Violet watched her go before she started up. Trafalgar offered her hand, which Violet took and allowed herself to be led.

Neither of them said anything until they were in Trafalgar's bedroom with the door closed behind them. Violet went to the bed and stood looking down at it, as if she was using her power to see what might happen there.

"This is only about sharing a bed," Trafalgar whispered.

Violet said, "Is it? It seems as if Beatrice assumed we were going to be getting up to something. An idea she probably got from Lady Boone."

"Just because they assume something~"

"No, I..." She cleared her throat. She looked up. "I want it to happen. And if they're going to assume it happened anyway, it would seem like a waste to deprive ourselves."

Trafalgar closed the distance between them. "I wouldn't want to be accused of something I hadn't done." She held eye contact as her fingers found the catch of Violet's trousers. Violet breathed in deeply and almost blinked, but kept her eyes open. "Are you sure about this?"

"I'm sure that we have no guarantees." Violet reached up to start unbuttoning Trafalgar's blouse. "Tomorrow we could be struck down by a mysterious illness or stepped on by a giant. I'm sure that finding someone you care about, who cares as much about you in return, is too rare to ignore." She finished with the last button and slipped her hands underneath, sliding them along Trafalgar's waist. "And I'm sure that no matter what is about to happen, there's only one outcome that I would regret."

"Fantastic."

They kissed, and Trafalgar cupped Violet's rear end with both hands. A gentle push by Violet was enough for her trousers to collapse around her legs. She backed up and Trafalgar eased her down onto the mattress, breaking the kiss to stand above her and look down. Violet seemed to be holding her breath as she looked up, her focus dropping from Trafalgar's eyes to the strip of skin exposed by her open shirt. Trafalgar improved the view by shrugging out of the shirt and letting it fall from her arms.

"I don't have the most experience with this," Trafalgar said, "but I have learned some things from Dorothy and Beatrice."

"Dorothy *and*..." She looked toward the door. "You've been with both of them?"

"Is that a problem?"

"No." Violet's voice was small. "They're both so... so beautiful, Trafalgar..."

Trafalgar nodded. "Yes, they are. They both shine so brightly." She bent down and pressed her lips to both sides of Violet's mouth. "But you, Violet, are blinding."

Violet kissed her, let her hands roam, and slid her feet across the carpet as Trafalgar knelt down in front of her. She felt the tremor in Violet's hands and reached down to bring them to her mouth. She broke the kiss and sat back on her heels, closed her eyes, and gently kissed her way down the fingers of one hand until she reached the palm.

"If at any time you want me to stop—"

"I won't want that," Violet said breathlessly. "But... ah... if... I need you to slow down..."

Trafalgar said, "You can tell me. We'll move at your pace. Is that all right?"

Violet bit her lip and nodded. There were tears in her eyes. "For now, though, you can hurry. I-if you want."

Trafalgar smiled and bent down. Violet leaned back so she could see what was happening, her breathing fast and irregular. Trafalgar kissed one thigh, then the other, then she moved the damp material out of her way to kiss between them. Violet tensed with a gasp, then relaxed, and her legs tightened around Trafalgar's body. She put her hands on top of Trafalgar's head and left them there, one on top of the other, moving her hips in concert with the movement of Trafalgar's tongue.

"Hurry, hurry," Violet gasped.

Trafalgar wasn't entirely sure she was aware she was saying it out loud, but she still complied. Violet continued her chant, the same word, two rushed words with the stress on alternating syllables, a mantra that Trafalgar found useful to time her strokes. As she suspected, it didn't take long before she felt the first tremors of orgasm. She looked up, the angle pressing her tongue harder against the sensitive flesh, and watched Violet for signs that she wanted to retreat. But the look of sheer rapture on Violet's face - eyes closed, mouth open wide, sweating just enough in just enough light to make her forehead glisten - and she knew teasing would not be welcomed.

She used a trick Dorothy had taught her, which caused a scream that Violet cut off with a slap against her mouth. She grunted and slipped her middle finger into her mouth, bit down hard on it, and climaxed with a melodic growl of pleasure.

Trafalgar waited to be freed from the trap of Violet's legs before sliding up her body. Violet had collapsed, arms flopped at her sides, and barely seemed to notice Trafalgar kissing her breasts through her shirt. She came to her senses at the first kiss on her lips, which she returned with enthusiasm. She closed her legs again, this time around Trafalgar's waist, and pulled her in.

When the kiss broke, she looked at Trafalgar with half-lidded eyes. "*That* is 'not very experienced'? There are teeth marks on my finger."

"Shall I kiss it and make it better?"

"No! God, no, not yet. Gosh. Your kisses are fatal." She shuddered and laughed at herself, then kissed Trafalgar's lips. "That taste on your lips..."

Trafalgar said, "It's you."

"Gosh," Violet said. "My gosh."

"We should get some rest... let you recover."

Violet said, "No, no. I'm wide awake now." She rolled over and took Trafalgar with her. Trafalgar laughed and put her hands on Violet's shoulders. Once they were settled, she moved them down to cup Violet's breasts. Violet arched her back in response. "I would definitely like to feel that again. But while I'm recovering, I want to make you feel that good."

Trafalgar took a deep breath and raised an eyebrow. "I think I would like that very much."

"You may have to tell me what to do, though."

"Then by all means... let's begin."

## CHAPTER EIGHTEEN

DOROTHY WAS almost asleep in the bath when she heard a sudden cry cut off by a slapping sound. She opened her eyes and listened for more context noises, but none came. She sat up straighter and brought her hands up to draw more water across her breasts. It had been an exhausting day, and she'd barely done any of the actual work. After they brought Beatrice back to Threadneedle, she'd kept in contact with the various groups she'd sent out into the city. Some reported via telephone, others were tracked down by Sadie who would then run back to share the news with Dorothy.

There was no true census, of course, but from their own experiences they could extrapolate that there were hundreds, if not thousands, of magically empowered people. They used their newfound abilities to fight, steal, and cause general mayhem. It was her fault, yes, but she had no regrets. If the options were hundreds of thousands of people who could use magic for criminal endeavors or millions of corpses, she would make the same decision every time.

Beatrice slipped into the bathroom, lips twisted in a knowing smile. "Trafalgar and her new inamorata are here."

"Ah." Dorothy closed her eyes, then opened them and raised an eyebrow. She recalled the cry that had woken her. "Oh... you don't suppose..."

"Oh yes." Beatrice sat on the edge of the tub. "I heard them when I passed her bedroom earlier. I'd recognize the sound of those bedsprings anywhere."

Dorothy smiled. "Good for her."

"Sad for us."

"Quite," Dorothy agreed. "But perhaps our arrangement was never meant to be forever."

Beatrice said, "But it was very enjoyable while it lasted." She put her hand under the water and massaged Dorothy's thigh. "I'm sorry I left you, Dorothy."

"Hey." Dorothy leaned forward and hooked a finger under Beatrice's chin, forcing her to make eye contact. "You stop that. If anyone is to blame for what happened, it's me. I knew you were overextending yourself to protect the house but I never even considered your well might be running dry. I pushed you to the limits. I promise you, it will never happen again."

"Be that as it may," Beatrice said, "spending so long with the uncertainty, not knowing if I would ever wake... It must have been hell."

"Got a high opinion of yourself," Dorothy muttered, feigning a joke to hide her discomfort.

Beatrice snickered. "Yeah. I may not remember any of it, but I think I can paint a pretty good picture. You haven't been out of the country since the incident. I bet you barely even left this house. I can imagine you sitting at my bedside day and night, waiting for me to wake up."

"The Dov told you that."

Beatrice clucked her tongue and splashed water against Dorothy's chest. "She didn't have to tell me a damn thing. I know you." She paused and let the silence linger. Finally, she said, "Thank you. I've never had anyone wait for me like that. It's a nice feeling. To... to..."

"To be worth waiting for," Dorothy said.

"Yes."

It was Beatrice's turn to hide her emotion, twisting to look at the door as if she'd heard someone coming. Dorothy allowed her the ruse and remained silent until she had composed herself.

"I think I've come up with a plan to end this whole mess. But it requires you, and it may be asking more than you can give."

"Tell me. Let me make the decision."

Dorothy brought her knees up and leaned against them. "I know about the prophecy surrounding you and the other elementals. Four magical beings who represent the essence of fire, earth, water, wind. When the four of you are brought together, the prophecy says it will bring about a fifth element. Void. You told me that you thought it sounded like a bad thing."

"Void doesn't exactly sound pleasant."

"Very true," Dorothy admitted. "But I believe the void refers to magic. The four elements coming together to restore balance, which would mean~"

"The end of magic."

Dorothy nodded. "It stands to reason, don't you think?"

Beatrice shrugged. "I suppose, yes. But there's a problem with your plan. I'm the only surviving elemental. Lasair, the fire elemental, was killed by Virago, and I killed her. We never even found wind. Probably for the best."

"The prophecy said that if one elemental died, another would take their place. They are out there, somewhere, and all we have to do is bring them here."

"It's still very risky," Beatrice said.

"The last risk I took brought you back to me. That's not going to make me averse to risking more in the future."

Beatrice said, "Even if we tried this plan, how do you intend to find the other elementals?"

Dorothy smiled. "That will be the easy part. The woman currently testing the resilience of Trafalgar's bedsprings has a certain ability. She knows how to find things."

Another cry rose up from below, as if cued.

Beatrice couldn't help but laugh. "It would seem she does."

Dorothy grinned and settled back against the curve of the tub. "I don't know what will happen when the four elementals are reunited. It could drain what little strength you've built up. It might... it might send you back into the comatose state. But I definitely think it's the best plan."

"If you think it's the best option," Beatrice said, "then I agree as well. After all, risk is at the heart of everything we do, right?"

"Indeed," Dorothy said.

But now, for the first time, she considered the possibility of risk outweighing reward. There might come a time, very soon, when she would choose to just walk away and protect the treasures she'd already managed to find.

She trailed one finger down Beatrice's arm. Beatrice watched as if the water trail left behind in its wake was very interesting.

"Trix."

"Mm?"

"Please take off your clothes and get in this bath."

Beatrice didn't have to be asked twice.

In the morning, Trafalgar came downstairs and found Dorothy in the midst of preparing breakfast.

"Good morning," Dorothy said, trying and failing to conceal a smile. "Trix informed me that our houseguest decided to extend her stay. Will she be having breakfast with us this morning?"

"I believe she will. She's still asleep for the time being."

"I'll just bet she is, you beast."

Trafalgar smothered a smile of her own as she took a seat at the table, folding her hands in front of her. "Has there been any new information on our current predicament?"

Dorothy turned and gestured at the newspaper on the counter. "Typical bluster from the media. Unwarranted speculation, fearmongering." She poured a cup of tea and brought it over to the table, placing it in front of Trafalgar before returning to the stove. "The prevailing theory seems to be that this is a new evolution of the human species. We were always meant to gain powers, and this is just another change brought about by the reintroduction of magic to the world."

"It's an understandable conclusion, I suppose, the sudden outbreak followed by a seemingly spontaneous recovery, and then realizing you're not the same as you were before."

"Mm. I also spoke to Cora not long ago. There were a rash of burglaries all over the city, but most of them were stopped. Our new members really proved their worth last night. I told Cora that we would relieve them in about an hour."

"I shall inform Violet." Trafalgar sipped her tea. "I worry we're only seeing the first wave of consequences. Mere mortals are feeling the immediate effect, but that's only the surface. The Great War woke and empowered ancient, powerful forces that didn't make themselves known for years. Who knows what's out there building strength, biding its time..."

"Well, hopefully they won't have a chance to make their presence known."

"What's that supposed to mean?"

Dorothy brought over two plates of breakfast. She put one down in front of Trafalgar and took a seat across from her.

"I believe I've come up with a solution to the entire mess. And your new friend, Violet, plays a very important role."

She explained the plan she'd laid out to Beatrice, noticing Trafalgar's expression became grimmer rather than brightening. When she finished, she squared her shoulders and braced for harsh judgement.

"I'd ask what you think," Dorothy said, her excitement fading. "but your face is telling me everything I need to know. I've come back around to your way of thinking. We can undo the damage you believe I've done. Beatrice knows the risks and I believe now we can take measures to protect her before things become too dire. How is this not the perfect solution?"

"I hardly know where to begin," Trafalgar said. "Firstly, you have no idea what 'void' entails. You're only working on the assumption that it would be a solution to our current predicament. What if it makes things worse? What if bringing together the four elementals destroys all life?"

Dorothy scoffed. "Do you really think the power that makes Beatrice special could be that destructive?"

"I doubt the power is good or evil," Trafalgar said. "We see it as a force for good because Beatrice is a good person. We see it through her behavior, so we assume it's benevolent, but that is a naïve perspective. It would be like denying flames can destroy a house because the only one you've seen it is a fireplace. You are tempting fate."

"That is everything we do," Dorothy said, her voice rising with passion. "We tempt fate, we risk our safety to protect the world."

"And in doing so, we flood London with even more magic. A *third* wave of magic powerful enough to affect everyone within the city limits." She stood and began pacing. "We were asked to stem the tide, and instead you've taken a wrecking ball to the dam holding it back. I shudder to think about what we've set in motion trying to fix the multitude of mistakes we've made the past few days."

Dorothy twisted her lips and leaned back from the table. "I."

"Pardon?"

"What I've set in motion. The mistakes *I've* made the past few days. You've made it abundantly clear you don't agree with the choices I made, so you shouldn't take the blame."

Trafalgar pressed her lips together, then shook her head. "We're partners. Your mistakes are mine."

"I apologize for being a burden to you." She dabbed at her lips and stood up. "We never finished our conversation on this subject, so we might as well get it out of the way. If things had been different, and I'd been the one to enter the tomb to receive the banshee's curse, would you have used the former Elephants to cure me?"

Trafalgar remained silent, still, and kept her eyes locked on the floor. "I like to believe I would have exhausted every possibility before resorting to such drastic measures."

"I see."

"They are *women*, Dorothy, and you used them like tools!"

"I asked nothing more from them than I expect from myself."

Trafalgar said, "You still call them Elephants. You send them out like they're soldiers, expect them to push themselves to the limits until they end up like Beatrice."

Dorothy said, "How dare you. I was destroyed by what happened to Beatrice. To imply I would put anyone else through that–"

"You repeatedly struck Florence in the face to achieve your goal. You put her in the exact same situation with identical risks without blinking an eye."

"If you're implying I'm not tearing myself apart over that–"

"I think you are dangerously close to an ends-justify-the-means mentality, Dorothy, and that is a version of you that terrifies me. And if you want a more definitive answer from me, then no. If you had been lying in that bed, and the only way to save you was endangering four other lives, I would not do it."

Dorothy took a step back. Trafalgar stood her ground, but had the grace to look guilty. The silence hung between them until the sound of hesitant footsteps in the hall announced Beatrice's arrival. She stayed in the doorway and looked between the two women, waiting for one of them to be the first to speak, but neither seemed willing.

"Are you two finished?" Beatrice asked.

"Yes, I believe we are." Dorothy threw her napkin onto the plate and stepped around the table, almost bumping shoulders with Beatrice to avoid getting too close to Trafalgar. Beatrice watched her go, waiting until she was upstairs and behind a slammed door before she looked at Trafalgar again.

"Would you have let me die, too?"

Trafalgar said, "Yes."

Beatrice nodded. "I understand. You might not believe it, but I do."

"We keep saving each other's lives. We put each other above everything else, and I can't help but wonder if there will come a time when one of us is saved only to witness the end of the world. Sometimes sacrifices are necessary."

"Right you are. I feel the same way. But here's the thing... it's easy to be the one saying 'let go.' It's a whole different beast to be the one walking away. Because when that's you? When it's your decision? Sacrifice can feel a whole lot like abandonment."

She turned and went after Dorothy, leaving Trafalgar alone in the kitchen staring at two unfinished breakfasts.

## CHAPTER NINETEEN

TRAFALGAR CLEANED up in the kitchen, giving herself an excuse to remain downstairs for a bit before she risked jumping into the fire again. Finally she could delay no longer, and she was curious to see if Violet was still asleep or if she'd heard the argument and was hiding, and she went back upstairs. Her bedroom door was open, which was surprising, but even more surprising was the sight of Beatrice sitting in the armchair near the window. Violet was sitting up in bed, her legs under the blanket but her chemise exposed. They both looked at the door when Trafalgar appeared.

"What's going on?"

"Beatrice was explaining the plan to me," Violet said.

Trafalgar took an angry step into the room. "She's *what?*"

"She needed to know," Beatrice said. "Unless you were planning to make the decision for her. That doesn't seem quite your speed."

Trafalgar worked her jaw, angry. She held a steady glare on Beatrice but spoke to Violet. "You're under no obligation to risk your safety~"

"It's not a risk," Violet said. "It's literally my gift. It's what I do."

"And if it's successful, you and the other women could lose those gifts. Did Beatrice explain to you that none of us has any idea what 'void' really means? That finding the other elementals could just make things even worse than they already are? My God, we're fumbling around looking for the quickest and easiest solution. We'll burn London to the ground trying to save the bloody place."

Beatrice said, "The alternative is to let everyone who just gained a power burn it down instead."

Violet leaned forward. "Trafalgar, I want to try. We have to try. Or, what, we keep running around London being the magic police? Deciding who is using their new abilities right and who is wrong? This is the way."

"Besides, magic existed before the Great War," Beatrice said. "I was born well before the first bullet was fired, as were the other elementals. Maybe there's some base level of magic that will always exist. We have to take the chance."

Trafalgar burned, knew they could tell how incensed she was, but she refused to get into another row that she was certain to lose. Beatrice was right. It was Violet's decision for how her power should be used. But they had already risked so much, and if something went wrong with this solution, how much farther would they be willing to go? Who would be the next person to put their head on the chopping block, and what would they be asked to give up?

"Do it if you must, but I won't be here to witness it." Trafalgar went to the closet and crouched to retrieve a leather satchel. She checked to make sure her preferred weapons were in it, then stood and slung the strap over her shoulder.

Violet started to get out of bed. "Wait, Trafalgar..."

"No. You have to stay here for their damned plan. I'm going to find the rest of the Society to see where I'm needed. There are no doubt fires which need to be extinguished. I'll inform the others about your plan. Violet... Vi." She looked at her, held her gaze, tried to let her know that her anger wasn't directed at her. "You can change your mind at any point. No matter how they try to push you..."

"I know," Violet said.

Trafalgar nodded, then looked at Beatrice. "Protect her."

"I will," Beatrice promised.

"Trix..."

"I will," Beatrice said again, stressing both words.

Trafalgar believed her. She looked at Violet again, put a hand over her heart, and turned to leave.

She was at the bottom of the stairs when she heard Dorothy's bedroom door open. She waited until she was at the door to look back. Dorothy stared down at her. She was as still as a statue. Trafalgar had a thousand things she wanted to say, and she could see an equal number of words in Dorothy's stare. Most of the words were hurtful, petty barbs that she knew she would never be able to take back. The rest were just repetitions of things she'd already said.

Finally, she spoke. "If she is hurt in anyway, I will hold you responsible."

Dorothy dipped her chin. "Understood."

Trafalgar turned her back and walked out of the Threadneedle house, uncertain if she would ever again walk back in.

The Rookery was half-empty that morning, with most crews on supply runs or pleasure cruises to the north. The hangars on the shore of the Thames looked abandoned, but the few pilots who were home that day took full advantage of the vacancies. Araminta Crook had scored a prime slot for her *Skylarker* due to all the vacancies, and she was taking full advantage of it. The cargo hatch was down and she'd stretched a length of netting across the opening to serve as a hammock. She had a drink, she had a baggie of special snacks she'd brought back from their last trip to Belgium, and she was halfway through a very gripping novel.

The book was currently lying facedown on her stomach while she "rested her eyes," moving her right foot just enough to make the netting sway. She was very close to being asleep when she heard someone enter the cargo hold. She stopped swaying, opened her eyes, and picked up the book. She blinked repeatedly until the words snapped into focus and she pretended she'd been reading the entire time.

"You know," her navigator Thabisa said, "snoring echoes very well through this space."

Araminta said, "Helpful information to anyone who has the misfortune of falling asleep here, I suppose, but utterly nonsensical at the moment."

"Mm," Thabisa said. "I just wanted to let you know I've completed the Hamburg route. Forecast looks like we'll have clear sailing the whole way. Should be nice and smooth there and back. Bit boring, in fact."

"Sometimes we like boring, Thabisa." Araminta began the not-so-simple process of getting out of her hammock. "We crave boring, we dream of uneventful days. May all our engagements be boring."

Thabisa said, "Aye, ma'am. I have the charts if you'd like to take a look at them."

Araminta dropped onto the deck and began stowing her things. "I trust you, but I'll take a look at them anyway. You have a certain way of making it fascinating."

She had just reached out for the log when a wall of water crashed into the open hatch, sending a tidal wave flooding across the deck. Araminta and Thabisa were both knocked off their feet. They were buoyed on the surface before their weight pulled them into the water, forcing them to swim even as it began to recede. Araminta dropped her satchel as she was swept across the floor. Thabisa tumbled past her and Araminta managed to curl an arm around the navigator's, hooking her elbow and twisting to pull the other woman tight against her.

When they swept past the net, the best Araminta could do was lift her feet so they were caught in the webbing. She twisted her ankle and looped it around her foot, then grabbed with her free hand until she got her hands on another section. Thabisa grabbed hold as well. Between the two of them they were able to hold on until the wave had fully swept back outside and they were dropped heavily onto the deck.

They both coughed violently, spitting up mouths full of dirty Thames water. The ship was still swaying from the force of whatever hit it, and the air was full of sirens and alarms from the other ships at the Rookery. Araminta reached out for Thabisa's shoulder, but her concern was waved off with another hacking cough. The captain got to her feet, also still coughing, and walked down the ramp to see if she could spot the cause of their sudden dousing.

The culprit was immediately apparent. Due east of the Rookery, heading toward the center of London, the water of the Thames was breached by the wide back of some sort of reptile. The sun glinted off its scales and the curved spines running down the center of its back. It lifted a diamond shaped head as if to scent the air, then dived again and sent another devastating wave crashing up onto the shore. Araminta watched as people gawping were knocked off their feet, and she prayed none of them were washed out into the river.

Thabisa joined her, still coughing but not quite as violently as before. "The hell is that?"

"I haven't the foggiest," Araminta said. "But I think we're about to start craving boredom."

"Is it just London?"

Cora's question wasn't directed at Trafalgar, but it was the first thing she heard as she came into the Inkwell. Cora had clearly been awake all night. She looked utterly wrecked, her hair undone and her focus uncertain. Trafalgar felt guilty to think of the work Cora had been doing while she and Violet were being so frivolous. Cora managed a smile and a nod, then turned back to the girl she'd actually been addressing; Sadie Halladay, the runner.

"As near as I can tell, mum," Sadie said. "I'm not too good at this sort of thing, but I talked it over with Rosetta. That's Rosetta Temple, she~"

"I know her." Cora explained to Trafalgar, "She was one of my girls. Went to university."

Sadie nodded. "Well, anyway, Rosetta says that since the original curse was probably focused on the 'center of power,' then it would only affect London. So the thing Lady Boone did to fix it would only hit London, too. We're kinda in the middle of a bubble here, maybe. But it's going to spread eventually. People will only stay in one place for so long."

Trafalgar said, "People may have acquired teleportation abilities. They could be traveling all over the world in seconds. If they can spread this around~"

Cora sighed. "We have no idea if that's possible, but it's something else we need to investigate. Is this an isolated event or will it become worse over time? Will it spread to Wales, Ireland…"

"*We* need to investigate it," Trafalgar said. "You've likely been awake for over twenty-four hours. Get someone to drive you home. I'll take over here."

"I can just nap upstairs…"

"Absolutely not. In fact, anyone who has been here all night is officially relieved of duty until they get some rest. We should be getting a fresh batch of workers soon…" The door opened as if the woman on the other side had been waiting to be called. "Speak of the devil."

Emily Tripp froze on the threshold. She looked around and said, "Pardon…?"

"Did you just get a good night's sleep?"

"Caught a few hours, yeah," Emily said.

Trafalgar nodded. "Welcome to the day shift. Night shift, you are hereby released. Go, rest, eat something. You're no good to the cause if you're worked to the bone." She tightened her grip on Cora's arm. "That goes double for you, Miss Hyde. You and Dorothy are often incredibly different but there are ways in which you are identical. Sleep. I want your word."

Cora patted Trafalgar's hand. "I swear to you, Miss Trafalgar, I will sleep. My body is already giving in, I think. I kept a detailed notebook about reports I've received, crimes stopped, empowered people we found or who found us. It was a very, very busy night in London." She suddenly looked at Trafalgar, then looked past her. "Speaking of which, where is Lady Boone? Beatrice, Violet. I half expected the four of you to begin traveling in a pack."

"Ah, we're… they will be here in their own time."

Mary Waterson put an arm around Cora's waist. To Trafalgar, she said, "I'll make sure she gets home safely."

"Thank you, Mary. And one more thing, ladies!" The group stopped to look at her. "No using your powers. Florence, Edith, Mabel, Honour, and Beatrice all pushed themselves to the very limits and nearly paid the ultimate price. We don't know if there's a finite amount of magic allotted to each individual, or if it will replenish itself in time, or…" She sighed. "There is too much we don't know. So for the time being, refrain from any unnecessary activity."

They nodded their agreement and began to file out. Emily made her way to where Trafalgar was standing, arms crossed over her chest. She waited until the last woman was gone before she spoke.

"I assumed you wouldn't want me to say this when all the others were still here, since it might've made it harder for 'em to leave. But they might see it anyway and come running back."

"Oh, god," Trafalgar said. "What is it?"

"I just come from the Thames," Emily said. "It looks like we've got a dragon."

## Chapter Twenty

Dorothy and Beatrice were in the parlor when Violet came downstairs. She wore one of Trafalgar's outfits, the shirt collar too wide and the sleeves rolled up past her elbows. She'd waited as long as she could but there was work to be done. She knew this next bit would be awkward, knew that following Dorothy's plan might endanger the new thing she was building with Trafalgar, but she was needed. It was her decision to make, and she believed Trafalgar was the sort of person who would respect that. She hoped, she prayed.

Dorothy had been seated by the fireplace and rose to meet Violet halfway. She cleared her throat, trying to look composed while her face gave away an inner anxiety.

"Are you certain you wish to go through with this? We won't hold it against you if you've changed your mind. I got the impression Trafalgar wasn't keen on you helping us with this plan."

Violet shrugged and put her hands in her pockets. "And I'm not terribly *keen* on people telling me what I can and can't do with my power. People have been doing it for too long, and I'm not about to go back to letting it happen now. I assume she'll understand this is my choice and respect that. You're certain this is the best course of action?"

"I do," Dorothy said without hesitation. "It's a good plan. And if it works the way I believe it will, we'll be doing exactly what Trafalgar and I agreed was necessary. It will bring magic down to pre-war levels and humanity can grow and evolve naturally on whatever path presents itself. It's dangerous and there are no guarantees, but that's true of almost everything we've ever done."

Violet had been convinced before she came downstairs, but it was still good to hear it directly from Dorothy. She nodded. "I'm ready."

"Splendid," Dorothy said, though it sounded like she was the reluctant one. She turned to Beatrice. "Trix, did you explain the prophecy to her?"

Beatrice said, "I gave her the gist. Four elementals. If one is killed, another is born to take her place. We know for a fact that two are dead. One of them is buried in the street out front. We never found the wind elemental, though we never really bothered to look for her, either."

Violet nodded. "So there's probably two babies out there somewhere..."

"We don't know that they were literally born," Dorothy said. "The mantle could simply be passed to someone else."

"It doesn't matter how old they are. I just need a general idea of what I'm looking for. I haven't failed yet." She looked at Beatrice. "So it'll be people like you? Really powerful, kind of just... making the air feel like buzzing all 'round you? Like that humming noise on the radio sometimes?"

Beatrice nodded. "Yeah. Back when Virago was trying to unite us all, we figured the elementals could be born anywhere but probably ended up drawn to each other. So if we're right, they shouldn't be terribly far away."

"Let's hope," Dorothy said.

Violet shrugged and pushed up the sleeves which had started slipping down her arms. "Well, okay then. Let's see what we can find."

"Do you need anything from us?" Dorothy asked.

"A little quiet, if you can manage it."

Dorothy arched an eyebrow and looked at Beatrice, who was covering a smile with her hand. Violet pretended not to see it as she closed her eyes. She rolled her shoulders, lifted her chin, and focused. She heard the end table drawer open and close as Dorothy retrieved a pad and pencil.

"Does it matter which one I find first?"

"No reason it should," Beatrice said.

"Okay. Earth elemental, that's easy enough. Threadneedle Street."

The next one was a bit more difficult. She could feel the corpse of the water elemental pulling her toward the street. She could tell exactly how deep it was buried, its position, but she knew that wasn't the actual target. If the prophecy was right, there was another water elemental out there. Either a baby or an adult. Living, breathing, capable of helping in their fight. Still, the corpse could be helpful. Now she had an idea of what the other elementals would look like when she found them.

She imagined the city laid out underneath her like a carpet, as if she was dangling from the gondola of an airship. So many narrow, winding streets. Hundreds and thousands of people, but only one who was right.

She went higher so she could see the entire city of London. She knew she was still in Dorothy Boone's parlor but she felt the cold wind on her face as if she was floating in the air above it. The baggy clothes she'd borrowed seemed to wave in the wind. *Focus*, she told herself. The streets looked like cobwebs stretched across green fields. The Thames was a shining green-brown ribbon cutting through it all. And...

"There's something in the Thames," she muttered. "Something big..."

"We can focus on that later," Dorothy said.

Violet nodded. "New Malden." The words were out of her mouth before she knew what she was saying, before she was even truly aware of what she was seeing. But there it was, about twenty kilometers south of Threadneedle, a strong beam of blue light that seemed to shoot into the sky. Violet focused on it and envisioned herself descending toward the street. She had never been to New Malden, but she knew the rooftops, factories, and train tracks were exactly what she would see.

"An address," Dorothy said. "We just need to know where to find her."

"You don't have to. She's on the move. Coming here. Maybe not exactly here, but I think she's drawn to something here. Either way, she's leaving there and coming to us."

Dorothy said, "I suppose that's fortunate."

Violet said, "She's the water elemental. I'll focus on fire now..."

Having found one elemental, finding the next was almost effortless. The energy was red, and it shone brightly from~

"Twickenham. But she's also on the move. She'll be here before the other one."

Dorothy sounded breathless. "That's three. Perhaps we don't need your ability if they're all coming to us. If you need to rest~"

"No, no need," Violet said, "I can already see the last one. The wind elemental." Her eyes opened. "She's in an airship that's preparing to dock at the Rookery."

Beatrice said, "All the elementals are in the same city at the same time?"

"And moving toward each other," Dorothy said. "Trix, have you felt drawn anywhere in particular since you woke up?"

"Other than a general urge to join the fight, I don't..." She lifted her chin and her eyes widened. "The Tower of London. It's been on my mind constantly since I woke up. I thought I was just using it as a landmark, but if all the elementals are being drawn to the same place, that has to be it."

"We can be there in ten minutes." Dorothy turned to Violet. "Thank you for your help with this."

"I hope Trafalgar understands."

Dorothy started to say something, then looked at Beatrice. Something silent passed between them. Dorothy stepped forward and put a hand on Violet's shoulder.

"She's a good person. She's analytical. She understands that sometimes the people she loves will come to a conclusion different from hers. I don't want to sound too full of myself, but she ended something pretty special with us to pursue something with you. She wouldn't have done that lightly."

"I hope you're right."

Beatrice said, "She usually is. It can be infuriating."

Dorothy smirked and squeezed Violet's arm. "You've played your part in this, and we owe you greatly. But now you should go to her. Be at her side for this. That's what she'll remember when the dust settles."

"I hope you're right. I'm just grateful I could help. It feels wonderful use these powers to do some good in the world. I haven't talked with all the ladies, but a lot of us feel the same way. We're making a difference. Being useful. A lot of us never thought that sort of thing was possible."

Dorothy smiled and nodded. "That's fantastic. I believe now that we've gotten past the awkward transitional stage, we'll all start to see the benefits of this partnership."

Violet agreed, wished them well, and excused herself so they could get ready to rendezvous with the other elementals.

As soon as she stepped outside, she heard sirens and shouts of terror coming from the Thames. She still wasn't certain what she'd seen swimming in the river, but she knew it was certainly large and destructive enough to cause that kind of commotion. And she hardly needed her powers to know that Trafalgar would certainly be found at the center of all the mayhem, but she still closed her eyes and reached out.

Trafalgar's energy was already familiar to her, and as comfortable as home. She smiled, basked in how it felt for a long moment, then descended the steps and hurried off to join the battle.

Dorothy donned a flat cap and round sunglasses for their excursion, following Beatrice out of the townhouse. She wished she had the time to fully appreciate this feeling. It was just as it had been in the old days, when it was just the two of them. She loved Trafalgar dearly, and their partnership had changed every aspect of her life for the better, but there was something wonderful about seeing Beatrice in her dark suit, jacket flapping behind her, shining shoes smacking the pavement as she cleared a path for Dorothy to follow behind her.

They ran the whole way to the Tower despite knowing there was no chance the other elementals could get there first. Even if they did, it was likely they would remain there even if they didn't know who or what they were waiting for. Dorothy didn't want to risk missing them and wanted to be in place as soon as they started showing up.

"There was a man," Beatrice shouted over her shoulder. "When Virago first suggested finding the other elementals. He warned us... he said that we would clear the path for something utterly loathsome. A vile situation that magic could prevent."

Dorothy said, "You're telling me this now?"

"I told you at the time. I'm just making sure you remember."

"We'll cross that bridge when we get to it. This situation, this threat, the current world is our focus from here on out. The future is an unknown country that we shouldn't waste time fretting about. It can only cause second-guessing and wheel-spinning. Good or bad, the future will arrive in due time. And that is when we will deal with the threats it brings."

"Sounds like a plan."

"Good. Now, let's... stop talking for a bit, hm?"

Beatrice laughed and nodded. She barely sounded out of breath, while Dorothy was panting. She'd gotten out of practice during those months sitting at Beatrice's bedside. She would have to get back into training when all this was over.

She'd expected the normal crowds around the Tower, but everyone's attention seemed to be on the commotion happening farther down the Thames. She could still hear the sirens, and now there was a distinct sound of destruction and echoing screams. She was sure Trafalgar and the rest of the Society could handle whatever was happening, but she hated being out of the loop almost as much as she hated running in the opposite direction.

They arrived at the white stone turrets which flanked the Tower's entrance, the modern additions blending surreally with the ancient structure. Normally she would have expected to see men in period uniforms standing guard, as well as students and people on holiday, but they seemed to be completely alone. The gates were locked tight and the bridge leading into the Tower was completely abandoned.

"Guess there's more exciting stuff to see right now," Beatrice said, also noticing how isolated the place was.

"Do we have to get inside?" Dorothy asked.

Beatrice shook her head. "No. Now that we're here, I feel... like I'm waiting." She turned in a full circle and looked around. She brought up one hand, spread the fingers, and stared at it. "And I can feel them coming. There's a charge in the air, like a storm is about to break."

Dorothy tried to feel it but couldn't, although she did feel something unusual. She attributed it to the amount of magic unleashed into the world in the past few hours. The ground shook under their feet. She thought she heard the crack of gunfire. Trafalgar was there. The Society was there. They had the situation completely under control.

"We'll wait," she said to Beatrice.

Beatrice nodded, also looking into the distance as if she could see what was happening.

The ground shook again.

## CHAPTER TWENTY-ONE

THE CREATURE wasn't, necessarily speaking, a dragon. Trafalgar wasn't entirely sure of the classification requirements, but she felt a dragon would have the ability to fly. The creature she was facing had no wings and seemed uncertain about moving on land, swaying under its own weight as it ambled down the stone street. It stood taller than any of the buildings and was just wide enough to fit down the street... barely. Each of its four legs had two flat talons at the front and a curving, hooked talon at the heel. The head was diamond-shaped and smooth, like a serpent, and the scales running down its length looked as hard as armor. Perhaps it was foolish to fit a creature they'd never encountered before into a single biological genus, but one thing was certain.

When she told this story in this future, she was absolutely going to call it a dragon.

She'd been joined by several other Society members after leaving the Inkwell, and they stood alongside her. To her right: Zilla Beverly with her sedative spikes, strongwoman Angel Tuffin, and Eveline Barrington, who was armed with a crossbow to utilize her marksmanship skills. To her left: Madge Sharp's fire manipulation, the unbreakable Isabella Stannard, and the winged Emily Tripp. People were still evacuating from buildings on either side of the street. They screamed in terror when they saw the creature, increasing the general panic of the situation as they fled.

Zilla looked at Trafalgar. "You're the monster-fighting expert here. Any words of advice?"

"Steer clear of the part with the teeth," Trafalgar said. "Everything else is improvisation."

"Swell," Zilla said.

The dragon flooded the street when it hauled itself from the Thames, and the dirty water lapped against their shoes as the creature slumped forward. Its neck was constantly in motion, swinging the heavy head back and forth like an enormous pendulum. Trafalgar couldn't tell if it was blind or merely trying to take in a multitude of alien sights all at the same time.

Eveline brought the crossbow up and lined up a sight. "I say we take it out now, 'fore it causes any other mayhem."

"Are you certain that bolt will pierce its scales?" Trafalgar said. "Or can you guarantee you'll hit the throat, the eye, inside the mouth, or some other fleshy area? Because if not, you're more likely to just anger it."

"I can hit wherever I aim," Eveline said, but she still lowered her weapon. "It's my thing."

Madge said, "You know for a fact it's not already angry?"

"All the damage it's caused so far is incidental. It's most likely confused and lost. Our goal should be sending it back to the Thames where it will be less of a threat." She pressed her lips together and stared up at the beast. She estimated it was at least seven meters tall at full stretch. "I am currently accepting theories on how we might be able to do that."

Angel said, "Zilla knocks it out, I drag her back to the water."

"Can you move something that large?"

Angel shrugged. "Give me enough time."

Trafalgar said, "Unfortunately time is not something we have in abundance."

The dragon shuffled forward again, upsetting its balance, and it swung hard to the side. It clipped a building and shattered the windows. Shards of glass and brick dust showered down onto the street. Trafalgar covered her eyes to avoid the dust and decided they couldn't dismiss any potential plans at the moment. She opened her mouth to tell Eveline she should try taking the shot when she was interrupted by the sound of an approaching car engine. Plenty of people were using vehicles to run away, but this one sounded like it was coming closer. She turned and saw a sedan rolling toward them. It was packed with women, but Trafalgar only knew one of them by sight.

Violet was at the wheel.

"The cavalry!" Angel shouted.

"So it seems!" Trafalgar agreed.

Violet climbed out of the car and Trafalgar ran to greet her. They gripped forearms as a substitute for the greeting they truly wanted to share.

"Need a hand?" Violet asked.

"A little help is always welcome." She looked at the other women who had gotten out of the car and were gazing up at the dragon. "You'll have to introduce me, I'm afraid."

"Phoebe and Pamela Read," Violet said, pointing at the two identical women Trafalgar had seen around the Inkwell. "Twin sisters. They sing harmonies to influence people. And Kathleen Farlow can create illusions."

The gears turned in Trafalgar's mind. To the twins, she said, "Can your harmonies work on something like that?"

They looked at each other before answering. "We've never tried~"

"~on anything that large~"

"~or non-human."

"Maybe," they concluded at the same time.

Trafalgar said, "This is a day when 'maybe' can be as good as a vow. Miss Farlow..."

"Any illusion you need, big or small as you'd like."

"Fantastic. With me!"

Eveline had concocted a new plan. She brought up her crossbow and aimed, holding, biding her time. As Trafalgar brought the new arrivals forward, the dragon lifted its foot to take a step. Eveline fired toward the ground at a steep angle. The bolt glanced off the stone of the street and ricocheted up across the front of the dragon's raised foot. The beast hissed and withdrew the leg. The thick neck twisted and looked down for the source of the irritation.

"Excellent idea!" Trafalgar said.

"It won't hold her off for long," Eveline said, "but for now she seems to be rethinking her route."

Trafalgar said, "Well, let's give her a detour, shall we?" There were two roads branching off to the east and west. "Does anyone know which road will take our new friend back to the Thames?"

Violet pointed. "That way. But I can't guarantee it will be wide enough for her the entire way."

"We'll deal with that problem when and if it arises. For now, with me!"

Trafalgar ran, and the women followed. It amazed her to think that less than a year ago, these women had been her enemies. Zilla had seemed ardent about the idea of being the one to kill her. Now they were following her into battle without question. Time could bring about all sorts of unexpected changes, a thought which made her turn to look at Violet. Violet didn't slow down but turned to meet Trafalgar's gaze. She smiled.

The first gunshot sounded like a branch cracking underfoot. Violet dropped to her knees and Trafalgar immediately changed course, running to her, panic seizing everything in her chest as she grabbed Violet's shoulders.

"Where are you hit?"

"What?" Violet grabbed Trafalgar's arm. "What are you~"

Another shot rang out. This time Trafalgar was able to locate its origin, even with the echo. A man stood in the doorway of a bakery, currently reloading his rifle. He brought it up and aimed at the dragon's throat, pulling the trigger and rocking back with the recoil. The slug bounced off the dragon's armored scales. The noise, however, had irritated the beast. It opened its mouth wide and let out a screech that made Trafalgar's ears ache.

"I'll show ya, beastie!" the man shouted. "I'll show ya not to~"

Angel grabbed the man, lifted him off his feet, and bounced his head off the top of the bakery's door frame. He went limp and she dropped him on the stoop, yanking the gun out of his hands. She turned to Trafalgar with eyes like a puppy expecting to be scolded for soiling the carpet.

"Sorry 'bout the violence."

"You did the right thing," Trafalgar said. "In this instance, at least. Not always, but... yes. In this instance." She looked at Violet again, cupped her face. "I thought you were hit."

Violet shook her head. "He was aiming up. I was just startled. I was startled by the noise, love, I'm sorry."

Trafalgar pressed her forehead to Violet's and closed her eyes, holding on to the moment before she got back to her feet. She offered her hand to Violet to help her up as well. Now that the unexpected distraction was dealt with, she became aware of a low, not unpleasant warbling sound reminiscent of birdsong. She searched the skies before realizing the sound was coming from the Read twins. It took her another few seconds to realize they were mimicking the screech the dragon had made. The beast lifted its head in response, eyes half-closed, and seemed to be trying to make sense of the noise.

"Miss Farlow!" Trafalgar shouted. "Create the illusion of another dragon moving toward the Thames!"

Kathleen dipped her head in acknowledgement and raised both hands. She aimed one at the dragon's head and the other down the street. She concentrated, baring her teeth with effort. Trafalgar scanned for evidence the illusion had been created, but she saw nothing.

"Where is it?"

"We can't see Kat's illusions unless she directs them at us," Emily said. "Keeps things less confusing in the heat of the moment."

Madge pointed. "It's working, though. Look!"

The dragon was moving again, feet still plodding along but with purpose now. The Reads continued their song, the melody rising and falling with their breath. They seemed to have found the right note and were holding to it. Trafalgar motioned for the women to keep pace with the creature.

"Our mission is to prevent any more misguided heroes like the baker," she told them. "Our hope is to get this lovely thing back in the water without any further injuries."

So they marched at the dragon's pace, flanking it on either side, with the Reads out front with Kathleen to lead the way. Violet was with them as navigator, telling them when the road ahead was clear. When there were obstacles, Angel and Isabella were sent to deal with whatever the obstruction might be. Eveline continued her foot-sting trick to keep the dragon as close to the center of the street as possible.

"I have to say I'm a little disappointed with this," Zilla said. "All my life I dreamt of slaying a real dragon."

Trafalgar tsked and shook her head. "Any fool with a sharp enough stick can slay a dragon. It takes brains and cunning to tame one."

People had figured out what was happening and helped clear the way, lining up on either side of the street to prevent anyone from blundering into danger. The parade continued until, at last, they reached the banks of the Thames. The dragon stood still and looked out at the water, suddenly hesitant. Kathleen was out of breath, her face shiny with sweat, and frowned up at the beast.

"I don't know what it's doing," she said. "I sent the fake dragon into the water. It should just dive on in."

"Let's hope it doesn't actually dive," Trafalgar said. "There will be enough of the river displaced if it's a gentle immersion. We don't need to drown Blackfriars just to get it back in the tub."

Violet looked east. "Oi. We may have a hand with that. More reinforcements."

Trafalgar turned and followed Violet's finger up. They weren't just receiving more help, the assist was coming from a familiar corner. She would have recognized Araminta's ship anywhere. She smiled and waved her arm in greeting.

"Ahoy, *Skylarker!*"

The ship blew its horn as it moved into position overhead. The cargo hatch was down and a member of the crew - she thought it was Luan, but whoever it was wore a leather cap and goggles against the wind - stood at the very edge of the safe space and saluted them. A thick rubber cord anchored the crewmember in place as they threaded a chain through their hands. The ship moved into position and the chain was thrown down, spiraling through the air to slip around the dragon's head.

The dragon reared back, balancing precariously on two feet. Trafalgar shouted, "Angel! Now!"

Angel rushed to action, slamming her full weight into the dragon's foot and rushing it forward. The dragon toppled, the chain went taut, and the *Skylarker* groaned under the strain of staying in the air. It was a perilous tug-of-war, but the ship won. The dragon went over the safety railing and the airship was able to slow its descent so it was dunked rather than crashing. The waves slapped over the banks but the Mnemosyne Society members were the only ones who were caught in it.

Trafalgar grabbed Violet's arm to keep from being knocked down by the force of the splash, laughing as Violet pulled her into an embrace. The other women laughed and applauded their successes, then turned to see the *Skylarker* repositioning itself on an eastern trajectory. It would be a long trip to the North Sea, but Trafalgar knew Captain Crook was capable enough to succeed without causing any further destruction.

"Tell your captain we owe her a drink!" Trafalgar shouted.

The crewmember saluted again, bowed, and then retreated back into the ship as the hatch closed. Trafalgar turned and looked at Violet. The waves of her hair were limp and darkened by the wave, and she was blinking the water out of her eyelashes. She looked like she had been salvaged from a sinking ship, but she was radiant and smiling, and her laughter was like music.

"We fought a dragon together," Trafalgar said.

"Yes." Violet clutched Trafalgar's collar. "I want you by my side for every dragon I face in the future."

Trafalgar remembered the seizing in her chest when she thought a bullet had abruptly ended their relationship. She nodded and fought back tears.

"I would like that very much, love."

A shout went up behind them. Trafalgar's smile faded as she turned toward it, half expecting to see some new threat had arisen. Instead she saw shop owners had ventured back out, wading toward them through the receding floodwaters. Every face that wasn't smiling was slack with awe, and the majority of people were clapping their hands.

"Hail!" one man shouted, and a few others echoed him. Soon it became a rallying cry. The man who started the cheer reached Trafalgar and clapped his hand against her shoulder. She saw ink stains on his hands, pencils tucked into his shirt pocket, and deduced he was a member of the press.

"Amazing work!" he said. "Truly amazing! Who do we have to thank for this salvation?"

Trafalgar smiled. "The Mnemosyne Society, sir. Allow me to spell that for you..."

## Chapter Twenty-Two

Dorothy and Beatrice didn't have to wait long for the first elemental to arrive. She was a tall, muscular African woman, her head shaved at the sides but kept long on the top. She paused when she came around the corner but only for one beat. Beatrice pushed away from the iron fencing she'd been leaning against and stood up straighter. The woman wore flowing purple slacks and a purple top made of a shimmering lightweight fabric. Her arms were bare to reveal tattoos marking her from wrist to shoulder. When she was close enough, Dorothy was able to determine they represented an ebbing tide.

"Kumona Majambu," the woman said when she arrived in front of Beatrice.

"Bao Tai Sek." Beatrice furrowed her brow. "But I go by Beatrice. Or Trix."

Kumona looked at Dorothy. "She is not one of us."

"No," Beatrice said, "but she's a friend. An ally. We can trust her."

"It's wonderful to finally~"

"The others should be nearby," Kumona said, not so much interrupting Dorothy as refusing to acknowledge she had spoken at all. "I can feel them."

Beatrice nodded. "Me too. May I ask... you haven't always been the water elemental. There was another. Her name was Emmeline Potter."

"I am unfamiliar," Kumona said. "But you are correct. My powers were awakened several months ago. But I was told for my entire life that I was intended for great things. I was stillborn, a tragedy. When the doctor laid my body aside, I began to breathe on my own. My grandmother said it was because God had designs on my life. I believed the day had come when I brought rain to a drought-stricken farm. Now I believe this was the day I have been waiting for."

"I believe you are correct."

Dorothy expected anything she had to say would simply be ignored, so she remained silent and looked toward the river. She spotted the airship and, a moment later, recognized it as the *Skylarker*. People closer to the banks were exclaiming and shouting about something. She could have sworn she heard the word "dragon" more than once. The commotion upriver had died down, and she assumed it had something to do with the airship's slow progress toward the sea.

"Trafalgar is certain to have an interesting story to tell later," Beatrice said.

"Quite," Dorothy said, hoping she was invited to the telling.

A few minutes after the *Skylarker* floated out of sight, another woman arrived. Her clothes were covered by a man's overcoat, buttoned all the way to her neck and the collar turned up. Dark blonde curls poked out from underneath her cap. She walked briskly, swinging one arm while the other remained tucked close to her side. Her upper lip protruded over the bottom, highlighting a weak chin and a strong nose. She eyed Dorothy even though she walked straight to Kumona and Beatrice.

"*Russki?*" she asked.

"English seems to be best," Kumona said.

The Russian grimaced but nodded. "Oksana." She looked at Dorothy, narrowed her eyes with suspicion, then widened them. "Lady Dorothy Boone...?"

"Yes," Dorothy said. "Have we met?"

Oksana suddenly brightened, striding directly to Dorothy and extending her hand. "I have read much about your exploits. I have a map you created framed in my study. The intrepid Lady Boone! Every time someone tells me 'ladies do not do such things,' I tell them no! One lady does in fact do these things all the time! You have silenced the clucking tongues of many men, Lady Boone! I never imagined you were one of us."

"She's not," Kumona said. "She is the dogsbody of this one. Bao Tai Sek."

Oksana said, "Oh, I see. Apologies, Lady Boone."

Dorothy waved off the apology, and decided she might as well let them think she worked for Beatrice.

Oksana walked back to the others. "As I said, I am Oksana Vengerov. I control flame. You are water," she said, nodding at Kumona's tattoos.

"Yes," Kumona said, introducing herself again.

"Earth," Beatrice offered. "Bea~ Bao Tai Sek."

"So we are lacking the breeze," Oksana said.

Beatrice said, "She was also missing the last time we were nearly united."

"She's coming," Oksana and Kumona said in unison, then looked at each other in surprise.

Beatrice nodded. "I can feel it, too."

Kumona folded her arms behind her back. "Perhaps while we wait, you can explain what we are doing here. The woman who explained my markings indicated meeting you would be a very bad idea."

Dorothy cleared her throat. "The past few days has seen London flooded with immense levels of magic. It has resulted in ordinary citizens gaining unbelievable powers, and that may only be the tip of the iceberg. We're teetering on a precipice that was created when we opened the well in the Great War, stealing access to power we were never meant to have. I believe the four of you exist as a countermeasure to bring things right."

Kumona nodded and looked around slowly as if trying to locate the source of a bad smell. "London does seem off. The air is..."

"Thick," Oksana offered.

Beatrice said, "Like there is a constant downpour of ash that you can't see but you feel it all over yourself."

Kumona nodded emphatically. "Yes."

The three elementals all turned at once, as if they'd all heard their names called, and Dorothy followed their gaze. A woman was striding toward them, her face obscured by a scarf which wrapped around the lower half of her face. Her skin was dark, her eyes black, and her thick eyebrows were knit together in an expression of anger or confusion. She walked to the others and examined each one in turn. Finally she yanked down the scarf.

"We should not be here like this." Her voice was thickly accented, and her eyes narrowed as she spoke. "It is incredibly dangerous. If the four elementals are ever united~"

"We create a fifth," Beatrice said. "The void. We believe that means we can put things back the way they're supposed to be. Magic shouldn't have been awakened. And London definitely should not be the magical capital of the world. We fear things will continue to spiral out of control if left unchecked. This is why we exist. It's what we were created to do."

Oksana said, "Then why call the fifth elemental void and not 'balance'?"

Kumona shrugged. "My native language is Kikongo. Between that, Russian, English..."

"French," Beatrice corrected.

"And..." She looked at the wind elemental, who hadn't offered her name.

"Farsi."

Kumona said, "There is bound to have been mistranslations. Perhaps it was always meant to be balance. Perhaps it was a lost word which means to wipe a slate clean. Whatever the truth, we are here now. We were drawn to this spot. There has to be a reason for that. Lady Boone's theory sounds as good to me as anything else."

Oksana shrugged. "So? How do we do it?" She looked at the newcomer. "And what's your name? We all introduced ourselves. Oksana Vengerov, Kumona Majambu, Bao Tai Sek, Lady Dorothy Boone."

The last woman lifted her chin. "You may call me the wind."

"No," Kumona said, holding an unblinking stare.

The Persian woman's lip twitched. Finally she said, "Nasim Turan."

"Very good." Oksana clapped and squared her shoulders, looking at each of the others in turn. "Do any of you have the slightest idea how to proceed?"

Beatrice cleared her throat. "Yes, I believe I do. Dorothy... I'm sorry..."

Dorothy blinked, surprised to be addressed. "Whatever for?"

Beatrice moved to stand next to her. "I don't think the spell you cast woke me up. It recharged me, yes, but the more I think about it, the less it makes sense. I woke up because I was being drawn here. To this ancient place, to the heart of what makes London what it is. With these women. I know what has to be done. And... I am... so sorry that I didn't tell you, but I feared you would try to stop it if you knew what was going to happen."

"What are you talking about?" Dorothy's voice was weak, tremulous.

"The four elementals unite to create a fifth. We don't create void. We become it. We cancel each other out. We..." Her voice cracked. "We cease to be."

Dorothy grabbed Beatrice's shoulders with both hands. "No! God, I won't allow~"

Beatrice put her hands on Dorothy's face. They were both crying now. Kumona, Oksana, and Nasim were all respectfully ignoring the spectacle playing out in front of them.

"You were right. This must happen. London must be returned to its proper state. That is what we were meant for. The elementals were born to maintain balance in the world. We were waiting for this moment."

"Please," Dorothy said. "I just got you back. Don't leave me again."

Beatrice's thumb brushed Dorothy's cheek. "I believe we were given this time to say goodbye to one another. To say the things which might have otherwise gone unsaid. I love you, Dorothy Boone. Every step I've taken in my life was in pursuit of finding you. I can think of no better life than the one I shared with you."

"It's not over," Dorothy said.

"I'm sorry." Beatrice leaned in and kissed her.

Dorothy thumped her fists against Beatrice's shoulders as she succumbed to the kiss, eyes screwed shut in anger.

The kiss ended suddenly, far too soon for Dorothy, but when she tried to continue it, she discovered her hands were bound by thick vines. She looked down to find their source and saw that they had slithered like snakes from within the Tower grounds. More appeared, and Dorothy's attempts to evade being ensnared proved futile. The vines wrapped around her legs, waist, and arms, holding her tightly without constricting. She fought so hard that her feet lifted off the ground and the vines compensated.

Beatrice backed away, tears streaking down her face. She pressed her fingers to her lips and blew a kiss to Dorothy before she turned around to join the circle of women. They gathered close around her.

A vine attempted to wrap around her mouth, but Dorothy twisted her neck to avoid it. "Beatrice!" she shouted. "Trix! Wait!"

Beatrice kept her back turned. Then, finally, she looked back.

Dorothy sobbed. "I love you."

Beatrice's expression softened. "Oh, and I love you, Dorothy. With all I am." Then she turned away again.

The four elementals held hands. Dorothy continued to fight, kicking and arching her back in an attempt to get free. The vines raised her higher, almost a full meter off the ground, and their grip tightened. She could still see the four women, though now they were surrounded by a column of swirling fog. Dorothy watched as the cloud darkened and thin bolts of lightning began to flicker within it. Beatrice's shoulder was hit, and Nasim shuddered as a bolt lashed across the back of her legs.

The ground shook. Dorothy couldn't feel it, but there was a sound that would have echoed all across England. The cloud grew larger, darker, and now the women were only vague shapes within. Dorothy shouted Beatrice's name again, but she knew it was no use. Flames appeared in the column, as if caught in an interior cyclone. And then...

For a moment, Dorothy would have sworn that all the oxygen in London simply vanished. She gasped for air, lips parted like a grounded salmon, but found nothing. And then...

Like a punch in the chest, the air was back. Dorothy coughed and choked on it, clutching at her throat even before she realized the vines had gone slack. The life went out of them and she tumbled down, her fall slowed a bit by the mass of suddenly inanimate greenery underneath her. She slumped on the pile of vines. Her head ached, a dull and throbbing pain, but she forced herself to lift it and look toward the women.

They had become a column of flame. It danced and twisted around on itself. Briefly, she believed she saw the shapes of four women within the dancing tongues of fire, but it burned too bright to focus.

"Trix," she whispered.

The fire exploded outward. Its heat only touched her for a moment, but it was so hot that Dorothy wouldn't have been surprised if she suffered burns from it. She screamed and covered her head, then rolled over to see where the wave had gone. There was nothing to see, of course. The street was as it had always been, with awnings and signs slowly waving as if a particularly strong breeze had just passed by but was now gone.

"Beatrice," Dorothy said again, arms wrapped around herself, leaning forward as if she'd been struck in the chest. "Beatrice."

It was the only word she could possibly think of.

What else was there to say?

## CHAPTER TWENTY-THREE

TRAFALGAR WAS leading the group back to the Inkwell when the gust hit them. It felt like a heavy cloud of humidity, like rain and fire mixed together in a small and brief storm. She covered her eyes with one hand as Violet clutched the other and stumbled against her side. Trafalgar steadied her and looked back at the others, all of whom were in various states of discombobulation. Zilla had a hand to her forehead and a flat look in her eye. The Read twins were clutching to one another, silently looking into the other sister's eyes for signs of what had happened.

"What was that?" Angel said. "Felt like being hit with a stone, but it was water."

Madge said, "There was a scouring aspect to it, for sure."

Trafalgar had a bad feeling about what might have just happened. "Emily... show me your wings."

Emily frowned but hunched her shoulders. The white feathered wings spread out from the center of her spine, expanding through the slit in her shirts that had been made to accommodate them.

Violet seemed to understand Trafalgar's intention. She closed her eyes and said, "Dorothy is at the Tower of London. The dragon is making good progress toward the sea."

"What are you thinking?" Zilla asked. "Magic got wiped out, but we get to keep our powers for some reason?"

"Maybe not everyone. Or maybe Dorothy's plan failed. Perhaps the effects aren't immediate. We really have no way of knowing right now." She clutched Violet's hand. "We can discuss it when we get to the Inkwell. For now we..."

Something had caught her eye, causing her to trail off. The others turned to see what she was looking at and saw a naked man stumbling out of a shop. At first there was something silvery to his skin, and it was almost possible to see the shop window behind him. But as he stepped off the curb, he seemed to solidify. He had one hand to his forehead like he'd just woken from a bender. He straightened slightly and noticed the women, flinched, smiled, then frowned. He scanned their faces and noted their expressions ranged from horror to disgust to bemusement.

"Can ye see me...?" he muttered.

"As regrettable as it is to admit," Zilla said, "oh yes, in all your glory."

He swore and covered himself, almost tripping over his feet in an attempt to get out of sight.

"Interesting," Trafalgar muttered, looking around for signs of other magic loss. The women with her tested their own abilities as much as they could. Isabella Stannard cautiously tested her skin with the prick of a knife blade, but she didn't draw blood. "Come on. The sooner we're back at the Inkwell, the faster we'll be able to conduct more scientific tests to see if we've been affected."

They started walking again. Now that the threat had passed, they could take account of the damage the dragon had left in its wake. Claws created deep cuts in the pavement. Cornices and the brick facades of many buildings had been crushed or cracked. She stopped counting when she reached fifty broken windows, since the number was clearly much higher than that. More people had come out onto the street to view the wreckage.

"Trav," Violet said as they neared the tavern. "I'm scared. I've... well, a lot of us... when we gained powers, a lot of us let it define us. If we lose them..."

"Then you will still be the same cunning, clever women you were yesterday. There will always be a place for you in the Mnemosyne Society." She paused. "Also, did you call me 'Trav'?"

"Oh. Yes." She shook her head. "I'm sorry, I was distracted. I wasn't thinking. I heard somewhere you don't like nicknames."

Trafalgar shook her head and smiled. "With you, I don't mind so much. It would be my honor to be Trav with you."

Violet put her head on Trafalgar's shoulder and remained silent for the rest of the walk, though Trafalgar was aware that she would occasionally close her eyes and then mutter a random location, checking to see if her powers had abandoned her yet. She lifted her gaze to the rooftops, wishing she could see across town to wherever Dorothy had ended up. She wished she could see what had happened a few minutes ago.

She also hoped she could see Dorothy's face when all the dust settled and they knew exactly how much damage had been done. She was very interested to know if Dorothy believed it was all worthwhile.

Dorothy knew everyone else would reconvene at the Inkwell, and that was why she returned home to Threadneedle. The sound of her footsteps echoed in the empty halls as she wandered from room to room, uncertain of what she was looking for. Not long ago, this house had been overflowing with life and love. Long dinners together in the dining room, just the three of them. Long conversation about who would be sleeping in which room, and who would be sharing a bed. She'd spent those glorious days terrified that it would all come crashing down, that she had to hold tight or she would lose it, but she told herself he was just being paranoid.

Now, here she stood. Alone, lost, broken, and without the faintest idea of what to do next. She went upstairs and looked at the bed where Beatrice had spent the past long months. Healed, returned to her, only to leave again. She walked to the bed, which was once again hers, and sat down on the edge. She closed her eyes, maybe she dozed off, but at some point she opened them to see she was no longer alone in the house.

Riya Lennox stood in the doorway. She looked haggard, weary... disappointed.

"Get out."

"I came to congratulate you on a job well done," Riya said flatly. "Magic has been stifled. No more creatures clawing their way back from the dark past, no more spontaneous awakening of magical abilities in ordinary people. Magic has been put back to sleep and the damage caused by the Great War can finally begin to heal."

"Then why don't you look pleased? You got what you wanted. I did what you asked of us."

Riya walked into the bedroom and lowered herself onto the bed with a burnt-out sigh. "Because you were supposed to work together. Because the partnership of Trafalgar and Boone were vital to what we've built, and you threw that all away for the easy option."

Dorothy narrowed her eyes. "We're... we will still be partners."

Riya sighed and shook her head. "Everything that has happened over the past few days was done without considering the consequences. You didn't think twice before summoning the other elementals, an act with repercussions which may not be felt for decades. And in the end, all you have done is tamped down the outbreak of magic. It's still there, still easily attained. Nothing I did made a damn lick of difference."

"Then maybe you should have left well enough alone, damn it."

Riya snorted. "That's what you said to me when I first told you about this plan."

Dorothy flinched. "So you weren't lying before?" The question was angry but, when she spoke again, her voice quaked with unshed tears. "Please tell me that you were lying."

"What? About your longevity?" She turned to face Dorothy fully. "You stood at the center of two massive maelstroms of magical energy, Dorothy. You created an atomic bomb of magic and then stood in front of it as it exploded. Twice. The elementals are powerful enough to change the very nature of reality and you were close enough to feel the steam of it on your face. Do you truly believe you could come out of that unscathed?"

Dorothy bowed her head. "I don't want it. Please."

Riya stood and looked down at her. "This won't be the last time we see each other, Lady Boone. You'll hold me as a baby. You'll know me for my entire life. I want you to know that one day I will look at you like this, sobbing, and I will be glad. I want you to suffer."

"I could ensure your forebears never meet. I could banish Janya Lennox to Antarctica. I could destroy your life."

"Clearly. Look how well you've done with yours."

Dorothy bowed her head. "Everything I did, every action I've taken these past few days was to get back the women I love. All I've done is send them even further away than before. And it's all my fault? You bear no responsibility for what's happened?"

"I warned you about the overuse of magic. You still allowed Beatrice to overtax herself to the point of destruction. And even when you saw that, you still relied on the powers of the women you liberated from Maud Keaton's clutches. You drowned London in so much magic that you had no choice but to do it again. I shudder to think how far you would have gone without the warning."

"So. Now what happens?"

"Now, when the next major conflict happens, there's enough residual magic left in the world that people try to tap it again. Both sides, this time. And trust me, the villains in this particular conflict are not the sort of people that you want with this kind of power."

Dorothy said, "So I'll stop them. We will. The Society."

"And the wheel keeps spinning." She pushed a hand through her hair. "I should never have come here. I should never have thought you would be our savior."

"I'll add you to the list of people I've disappointed over the years."

"Think of how many more you'll add before you're done."

Dorothy seethed, opening her mouth to respond, but she was alone in the room. Riya Lennox was gone to whatever future she'd come from, and it seemed very unlikely she would ever be back.

"To blazes with you, then..."

She sighed and let her anger dissipate. Her shoulders slumped and the fight went completely out of her. She flopped back onto the bed and squeezed her eyes shut, hoping that when she opened them, the world would once again have some semblance to normalcy.

By nightfall, they'd determined that only about half of the Society's new recruits had maintained their powers. The confusion and uncertainty seemed to have smoothed over the ruffled feathers of Cecil's crew, and they mingled with the others as they commiserated over their losses. The Inkwell's common room was more crowded than it had ever been when it still served as a tavern, and soon conversation turned to everyone's various adventures. Cecil and Agnes moved behind the bar to serve drinks, and soon the gathering had the air of a party.

Violet was one of the lucky few to maintain her powers, and she remained close to Trafalgar's side for the whole night.

"Do you still have your room at the Keepings' boardinghouse?" Trafalgar asked.

"I do." She lifted her head and looked up. "I can spend the night there if you'd prefer privacy. I know you and Dorothy probably have a lot to talk about..."

Trafalgar shook her head. "Perhaps, but that's not what I was asking. Do you think I would be able to stay there with you for a while?"

Violet frowned. "You're not going back to Threadneedle?"

"Not yet. You're probably right. Dorothy and I probably do have much to discuss. But it's not a conversation I feel like having."

"You're welcome to stay with me as long as you need," Violet said.

"Thank you."

"And here I thought you were taken," a disembodied voice said from Trafalgar's side. "Or are you just adding to the harem."

Trafalgar rolled her eyes. "Ivy, in case I haven't said how wonderful it is to have you back..."

"I was doing a little bit of a census. Looks like the ladies here are the lucky ones. Almost everyone who gained powers because of the first spell lost them because of whatever Dorothy did to fix things. So I guess London is back to normal."

"Not counting any scars that might be waiting to make themselves known in the coming months and years," Trafalgar said.

"For the record," Ivy said, her voice moving away from them, "I've missed you, too."

Violet waited to be sure she was truly gone before she spoke. "Do you really believe that? About fallout from everything that's happened?"

"There must be," Trafalgar said. "People were given unimaginable powers, however briefly. There's no telling how much damage could have been done in the time between the spells. I'm certain we'll spend no small amount of time clearing the debris of what has occurred here."

She wrapped her arm around Violet and squeezed her, scanning the faces of women she had come to trust and respect.

"Fortunately it looks as if we will have plenty of help, no matter what trouble arises."

## CHAPTER TWENTY-FOUR

DOROTHY BEGAN spending every waking hour in the second-floor archives of the Inkwell, ignoring the sounds of people coming and going downstairs as she haunted the stacks. She dug out every book she could find that hinted at the elemental prophecy. She called in favors from her wide array of contacts. She extended favors to the Dov just to be lectured on everything the mystic knew. It turned out not to be very much, and what she did learn wasn't particularly helpful, but the search kept her mind occupied. Even better, it kept her out of the Threadneedle house, with all of its memories and ghosts.

She wasn't sure how many days had passed since Beatrice's loss. She no longer kept a strict sleep schedule, sometimes working until she fell asleep at the table. It could have been a week, or as much as ten days, when she returned from the stacks to find Trafalgar standing at the top of the stairs. She looked like she was likely to flee, and Dorothy wished she had that option as well. She was trapped here as long as Trafalgar was blocking the exit, and she refused to cower and hide in the stacks.

So she carried her books to the table and sat them down before she spoke. "Hello."

"It's good to see you, Dorothy. Although I have to say, you hardly look well. When was the last time you got a proper night's sleep? Or a change of clothing?"

Dorothy said, "I don't have time for that."

Trafalgar finally crossed the threshold and approached the table. "Surely whatever you're researching can wait. The threat has passed. We've all but confirmed that everyone who gained powers in the first wave lost

them in the second. You've earned a break. I haven't seen you or Beatrice in-
-"

"Beatrice is dead."

Trafalgar physically recoiled, taking a moment to regain her breath. "What? I saw her, she was... she'd recovered..."

"My plan killed her. That's part of what void meant, apparently. It wasn't the end of the world, it was the destruction of the elementals. They united to become a fifth entity and that-" She waved her hand dismissively in the air around her head. "Then they carried out my plan. I won. Huzzah for me."

"No one told me..."

"I haven't told anyone," Dorothy said, bowing over the book again. "I can't, not before I have an answer, not until I fix this."

"You could have told *me*," Trafalgar snapped. "Good lord, Dorothy, I love her too. You don't think I should have been told..."

Dorothy looked up and fixed her with a cold glare. "Perhaps if you had ever chosen to come home, you'd have seen the truth."

Trafalgar tightened her jaw. "I was trying to give you space. I thought, given our last conversation, you would appreciate a chance to cool down."

"You would be *dead* if I hadn't taken action. You and your new love, along with countless others. I was forced to make an impossible choice. I feel absolutely no guilt for choosing the path that ended with you alive."

Trafalgar gestured at the table. "And now what are you doing? Looking for another magical cure-all that can bring Beatrice back? What if that also has unforeseen consequences? Another spell?"

"If that is what it takes."

"You're spiraling, Dorothy. How far will you go to rebuild the world in your image?"

Dorothy slapped her hand down on the open book and stood up. "I lost Desmond. I lost my grandmother. I'm losing you. And Beatrice... if there's the slightest chance..."

"I doubt you forced Beatrice to go through with the plan. When Violet and I left, the two of you seemed to be firmly on the same page. She chose this, regardless of the outcome. What makes you think she would condone you taking even more risks to bring her back?"

"How can you give up on her so blithely?"

Trafalgar sighed. "I'm not giving up on anyone. I'm merely accepting that sometimes victory comes at a tremendous cost. We hurt. We grieve. And we move on."

Dorothy slammed one of the books shut. "You can move on. But we have both been brought back from the brink of death. Hell, we've been beyond the brink. We know death can be undone. Don't we owe it to Beatrice to at least *try*?"

Trafalgar stood. She looked at the array of books laid out on the table, her eyes sad. "You can do whatever you wish, Dorothy. But you'll do it without my help."

"Fine by me. I'm getting pretty used to not having your help. Just like old times."

"I suppose I should find more permanent lodgings," Trafalgar said. "I'll have someone gather my things from the Threadneedle house."

Dorothy nodded and turned away. "Probably for the best."

"Dorothy..."

"Just go," she said. "We have nothing more to say to one another."

For a moment there was silence, but then she heard Trafalgar's footsteps going back to the stairs. She stopped there for a long moment.

"Goodbye, Dorothy."

Dorothy didn't respond. Trafalgar sighed and started down the stairs. Dorothy remained standing until she heard the door open and close downstairs, at which point she collapsed in the seat and clapped a hand over her eyes as if she could press the tears back in. Her shoulders trembled with unshed tears, and her throat felt raw and dry.

When the episode ended, she wiped at her face and took a steadying breath. She turned in the seat and stared at the books she'd gathered. They all said the same bloody thing, covering identical ground with only the barest changes for language or cultural reasons. She was no closer to finding the answer now than she'd been when she started. And honestly, if anyone had a chance of saving Beatrice, it was the Dov. And she'd seemed to think 'void' was final, irreversible.

Dorothy swept her arm across the table, shoving every book and all her notes to the floor in an epic crash. The answers weren't going to be found here, sitting in a library, reading about what other people had discovered in the past. It was all speculation, myth, legend. She'd seen the elementals in action. She knew they existed. She knew their names. Kumona Majambu. Oksana Vengerov. Nasim Turan. Bao Tai Sek.

She stood and pulled her coat from the back of the chair, slipping it on as she walked away from the table. Trafalgar was right. She'd spent far too much time alone, hiding, wallowing in her grief. It was time to do what she did best. Explore, but with a purpose. She shoved her hands into her pockets and stopped walking as she felt something in them. They were filled, actually, with dirt. She pulled out two handfuls and watched as it sifted through her fingers and landed silently at the floor by her feet.

"What in the world...?"

She opened her hands to look at the dirt. No one had been in the room except for Trafalgar, and she hadn't gotten close enough to pull a prank like this. And what sort of prank was this, to fill someone's coat pockets with... dirt. A thought occurred to her.

"Not dirt," she said under her breath. "Earth."

She spun quickly to look behind her, as if she expected to catch the culprit, but the room was empty. The stacks were silent, shadowed. She closed her fists around the dirt again, shoved both hands into her pockets, and marched down the stairs.

The secret of the elementals was out there somewhere, and she intended to uncover it.

Even if she had to do it alone.

Violet was waiting in the courtyard, seated on a bench with her head turned toward some minor commotion on the street. She hadn't heard the door open, so Trafalgar took a moment to appreciate the sight. She wore a pale yellow suit jacket that complimented her strawberry blonde curls, currently pulled back in a frizzy puff, and a black skirt. She looked utterly marvelous, breathtaking, and Trafalgar was grateful to have a moment to shift from her conversation with Dorothy to this.

Whatever had caught Violet's attention passed, and she realized she was being observed. She smiled when she saw Trafalgar. Caught out in her staring, Trafalgar returned the smile and closed the distance between them. She stood and raised her eyebrows hopefully, but her pained expression revealed she could read the truth in Trafalgar's eyes.

"Perhaps she just needs time," Violet said.

"Maybe." Trafalgar reached out to link their arms, but Violet turned slightly to avoid her. "Violet...? Is something the matter?"

Violet lowered her head. "I can't help but feel responsible. I pursued you too ardently, even though you told me about your relationship. If I'd simply held my tongue, perhaps..."

Trafalgar cupped Violet's cheek. "Stop that. I was drawn to you as well. And you being here had absolutely no bearing on what happened between me and Dorothy. Whatever is happening now would have happened even if we'd never met. The only difference is that I would be a true wreck if you weren't here offering your support. But I don't want you to feel obligated to stay. If you need time to consider... there have been many great changes in your life recently, and you would be completely within your rights to take a step back and examine things from a distance."

Violet looked up into the sky. When she looked back down, there were tears in her eyes.

"Ever since I got my power, I've used it to tell other people where things are. And I think after all this time, it's the reason I found the place where I'm supposed to be."

Trafalgar blinked back her own tears. This time when she offered her arm, Violet accepted it without hesitation. They began walking with no particular destination.

"Perhaps my partnership with Lady Boone served the same purpose. I'm not the same person I was when we first joined forces. I think I've become more... relaxed, less rigid, more open to considering another point of view. Without Dorothy, I would never have imagined myself with another woman, romantically. I'm not only better at my chosen profession because of her, I'm a better person. A happier person."

"I'm sure you had the same effect on her."

"I don't share your confidence. She's... obsessed now. The guilt and grief are all she can see. Our conversation may only have added anger to the mix, which is never a good thing. I doubt she would accept any help from me at the moment, but hopefully there are enough people in the Society who will see that she's hurting and will reach out. Cora, without a doubt, will be there for her when I can't. The scars will eventually heal. Dorothy will come to her senses and I have faith we can be colleagues again... if not friends."

"What will you do in the meantime?"

Trafalgar sighed and raised an eyebrow. "That's an excellent question. I suppose I'll have to find temporary lodgings. I suggested to Dorothy I would give her space, but I didn't think very far past that proclamation. It seems I find myself homeless."

Violet said, "The ladies are already gossiping about you spending so many nights with me at the boardinghouse, after I spent so long 'recuperating' at Threadneedle. I'm worried having you move in permanently would only add fire to the flame."

"Oh! Violet, no... dear, I wasn't implying that you should take me in."

"And I wasn't denying you," Violet said. "I'm only saying that maybe it would be best, and more comfortable, if we found separate accommodations elsewhere. To-together."

Trafalgar raised an eyebrow. "That's a rather big step."

"Too big?"

"It's funny. I just scolded Dorothy for taking too many big steps. The truth is, we've both made a habit out of going too far without much worry over the consequences. But I think there's nothing big about this step. Scary, yes. But definitely the only path worth taking at the moment."

Violet smiled. They had arrived at the corner, and Violet stopped to bring Trafalgar's hand to her mouth so she could kiss the knuckles.

"Whatever happens," she said, "however this ends, and despite everything we've been through, I'm grateful. You told Leonard to 'never apologize for adventure.' I truly understand what you meant by that. I could have died. So many people could have died, or suffered horrible injuries, and yet this has been the best time of my life. I can hardly wait for the next adventure."

"It's bound to be just as deadly. Perhaps worse."

Violet smiled. "Fantastic."

Beyond Violet, Trafalgar saw Dorothy come out of the Inkwell courtyard. She paused and looked one way, then the other. She stiffened when their eyes locked. Trafalgar didn't blink or turn away. She returned the stare, even as Dorothy tightened her jaw and lifted her chin. There was too much space between them, literally and figuratively, for her to read what it meant.

After a long moment, Dorothy turned her back and walked away.

Trafalgar squeezed Violet's hand, put an arm around her, and walked in the opposite direction.

Miss Trafalgar and Lady Boone
will return for a final adventure
in
TRAFALGAR
VERSUS
BOONE

# About the Author

Geonn Cannon is the author of over fifty novels, including the Riley Parra series which was adapted into an Emmy-nominated webseries by Tello Films. He's also written two tie-in novels for the television series Stargate SG-1. He was the first male author to win a Golden Crown Literary Society Award for his novel Gemini, and he won a second for Dogs of War. Information about his other works and an archive of free stories can be found online at geonncannon.com.

**Prize Fighter**

Six years ago, professional boxer Max "Wrecker" Reszke lost control in the ring. One moment of blind rage puts her opponent into a coma from which she never woke. Though cleared of any criminal charges, Max hangs up her gloves and swears that she'll never risk losing control like that again.

Until one night, a chance encounter in an alley, a damsel in distress. Max leaps into action and saves the stranger. She soon learns that the woman she saved is actress Renee Lamar. Renee, anxious and paranoid about security, offers to reward Max's chivalry with a job as her bodyguard.

Max has nothing to lose by agreeing, but soon discovers Renee might be her own worst enemy. Half a decade after leaving the ring, Max faces a new fightthat can't be won with fists.

**Into the Furnace**

Kelly Lake comes from a family of firefighters, but she still had to prove herself to her brothers and her father before they accepted her as one of their own. On her days off she tends bar at the firehouse hangout across the street and spends time trying to breathe life into a relationship she knows is doomed. Her life is cruising along just fine until the day her squad responds to a horrific arson that will cause her carefully orchestrated balancing act to come falling down around her. The blaze claims the lives of eleven people, half of them children, and the fire department takes the blame.

Kelly soon finds herself at the center of a media firestorm when she inadvertently becomes the poster girl for the incident. The trauma of the fire is compounded by her personal house of cards collapsing. Her relationship begins showing its cracks at the same time long-buried family secrets rear their ugly heads. Attacked from all angles, Kelly starts thinking the only place she'll be safe is running headlong into the furnace.

*"Easily one of the best samplings of queer fiction I've had the pleasure to read in a very long time. I could not recommend it more, and sincerely hope that upon its release in November Into the Furnace will light the same fire in each of your hearts that it has already lit in mine." - Tabitha Beth, The Rainbow Hub.*